THE GUNSMITH

**Center Point
Large Print**

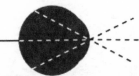

**This Large Print Book carries the
Seal of Approval of N.A.V.H.**

THE
GUNSMITH

LAURAN PAINE

CENTER POINT PUBLISHING
THORNDIKE, MAINE

This Center Point Large Print edition
is published in the year 2010 by arrangement with
Golden West Literary Agency.

The text of this Large Print edition is unabridged.
In other aspects, this book may vary
from the original edition.
Printed in the United States of America
on permanent paper.
Set in 16-point Times New Roman type.

ISBN: 978-1-60285-854-1

Library of Congress Cataloging-in-Publication Data

Paine, Lauran.
   The gunsmith / Lauran Paine. — Center Point large print ed.
      p. cm.
   ISBN 978-1-60285-854-1 (library binding : alk. paper)
   1. Large type books. I. Title.
PS3566.A34G885 2010
813'.54—dc22

2010016146

1

Spartanville

It has been said that in small communities the only way to keep a secret is to tell it first. While this may be true in established communities, it did not apply to places where the population in the aftermath of a war moved in, moved out and moved on. Dave Petrie had lived in Spartanville longer than most people, was a walking encyclopedia of his town and its events, and although an old-timer by any definition had to be old, Dave had opened his gun shop about a year after the Confederacy collapsed and he had turned his back, headed west, and didn't stop until he found Spartanville, which was founded the year he arrived, something like nine years before.

Dave Petrie had been fifteen years old when he enlisted in Fitzgibbon's Company A, 3rd Battalion, 4th Corps, General Jubal Early's Army of the West, Confederate States of America.

The war lasted a few days shy of four years. When Dave Petrie turned his back on four years of blood, struggle, hunger, sickening casualties and a ruined 'nation' he had been close to nineteen. When he arrived in Spartanville he had been a tad over twenty years of age.

He had settled in, had watched a buffalo-hunters

camp evolve into a tent-town with almost as many saloons as settlers, and to go on from there to become what it now was. A place of wooden structures, even a red-brick bank, shade trees, and an *acequia* that carried water from a river over two miles northeasterly through town on both sides of Main Street.

And Dave was now some shy of thirty, young for an old-timer who had only been shaving for about twelve years. Old in experience, in convictions, old only in the way wars make men old regardless of their age.

He wasn't particularly outstanding in appearance, being less than six feet tall, a little on the sinewy side in build with grey-blue eyes and an easy manner that went with his easy smile.

Like most men of his build, Dave Petrie was fast. There was a story about the time he opened the alley door of his gun works where a coiled rattler was sunning itself. Dave had seconds to raise the sole of his boot before the snake struck. After it struck, before it could coil to strike again he had it in his fist just behind the head, and killed it.

Old Man Bulow who operated a makeshift stage and cartage company across the road on the west side of Main Street told of another incident . . . and retold it as often as Dave Petrie's name came up.

It happened in the early days when Spartanville was a tent-town. A big, whiskered man named Plummer had come to town with three equally as fierce, faded, truculent individuals, and started a ruckus in the tent-saloon where the Spartanville rooming house stood later.

Plummer was a notorious outlaw and trouble-maker. Years later he would end up dead in northern Colorado at a town named Virginia Dale.

He elbowed the smaller, leaner man away from the bar by spreading thick arms and growling. Plummer made the same mistake others had made. Dave Petrie didn't look nor act dangerous, but he was.

He gave ground, which Plummer expected, but when the big bearded man turned to order whiskey from the barman, Dave tapped his shoulder. When Plummer turned a stone-hard fist caught him squarely in the mouth. Plummer did not go down but he hadn't expected anything. He raised his right hand to his bloody mouth, started to raise his left arm to protect himself, but the flurry of blows broke past the arm and peppered the large man until his knees buckled.

His hardcase companions were too astonished to get untracked until it was over, by which time it was too late. Only one of them went for his hol-stered Colt. The barman caught him a solid blow under the ear with an ash spoke.

The other two renegades looked around. There was not a friendly face looking back. They got their companions upright, supported them out to the tie rack and all four left town never to return.

Dave Petrie had learned a little about weapons during the war. He learned a little more from an old man, dead now, who had hand-made rifles and pistols in the Kentucky mountains years back, even before the war.

What else he had to know he taught himself until he became as good a weapons man as there was west of the Missouri.

The year he opened his shop he met a girl named Betsy Ann Miller. It was a source of local amusement the way he courted her. Like a cub bear, playful and awkward, tongue-tied and forgetful. When she ran off with a traveling drummer who wore grey spats and a little curly-brim derby hat who had what he swore was a genuine diamond stickpin, Dave rode off into the westerly mountains and did not return for more than a week. Folks understood and to their credit never mentioned Betsy Ann Miller when the gunsmith was around.

Being a small town inhabited by people who knew everyone else's business, they faced trouble of all kinds with a kind of kin-like unity. They had to; problems came to all of them when they arrived. They had no choice but to rely on one another. Spartanville had that almost-kinship attitude of most small communities in a large and generally otherwise uninhabited territory.

The nearest cattle ranches were miles distant, nor were most ranchers concerned with the town except as a source of supplies. There was no actual ill-will between townsfolk and stockmen, it was basically the difference between townsfolk and countryfolk—distance first, and no basic shared interests beyond periodic trade. There had once been a retired army surgeon in Spartanville, but he had died some years back.

While he lived ranch people visited town as often as their health required, and that was how most residents of the town got to know the countryfolk.

Spartanville had once hired a constable, but he had lasted only as long as poor pay, boredom, and the wandering instinct of his kind allowed.

In his place there was a vigilance committee to which most of the menfolk belonged. It had been mustered so few times that it had degenerated into a kind of social organization, sponsored dances, Christmas parties in winter, and cook-outs otherwise.

Winter in Colorado was always cold, usually with cluttering snow, and slackened-off trade, which resulted in Spartanville's residents going into a kind of hibernation.

It was springtime and summer when the town and its environs stirred to life.

Dave Petrie like most other folks had come to accept this periodic swing in weather and trade. As Gerald Shoup had once said to the gunsmith, there wasn't much difference between people in cold country and bears; they both had shortened vistas, stored fat and hibernated in winter.

Gerald owned the only saloon in Spartanville. He had built it several years before a Methodist Mission had come along seeking a site to erect a house of worship. The one they had built on as the most strategic site in Spartanville was directly across from Shoup's saloon.

The missionaries had not liked that arrangement and neither did Gerald, a greying, rawboned man of indeterminate years. For one thing Gerald had opened his saloon every Sunday morning for as long as he'd had the place. Once, the local preacher, a wispy individual with sharp, fox-like features named John Kent, came over to mention his dissatisfaction, but only once.

Gerald had told the minister he cared for his flock exactly as Reverend Kent cared for his flock, they both favored peace and goodwill, their approaches were different was all. Gerald's source of goodwill was liquid and the preacher's source was fairy tales.

Reverend Kent never entered the saloon again, would not nod or speak to Gerald Shoup except when it could not be avoided, and preached harder than ever against the evils of John Barleycorn.

If there was even mild dissent among Spartanville's inhabitants it was over this issue, and except for a few females who made them-selves obnoxious once in a while when the Lady's

Altar Society would parade on the Fourth of July carrying placards denouncing evil in all its forms, which was as near as they dared come in denouncing that boar's nest of happy evil their menfolk patronized, it was not really a divisive issue, it was more like a question of whose bull was getting gored, and since men had the last word in all disputes between the sexes, it was for the most part confined to arguments in the kitchens—and bedrooms—around town. When genuine problems came, such as floods or fires, this problem was forgotten.

It did not amount to a hill of beans anyway. Menfolk dutifully oiled their footwear, squeezed into their go-to-meeting attire and sat through Preacher Kent's fire and brimstone orations, and when Sunday service was over, they made a bee-line for Gerald's place.

These little sparking, sputtering dissents had to exist, if for no other reason because one sex sat down to pee while the other sex didn't. They were probably good for a community. When real trouble came, men and women pulled together like any good team of horses or mules. Ordinarily they were resurrected during the long, cold, housebound winters when folks got bored.

With the advent of springtime and summer, when muddy roads were again usable, trade and traffic picked up, as issues of importance they were forgotten.

It was late springtime with countrymen praying for rain and townsfolk praying it wouldn't rain, that Spartanville got a surprise it hadn't seen the like of before. An event that occasioned conversation summer and winter for years to come.

In earlier times after the war bands of marauders swept through the land, disenfranchised former Secesh and Union soldiers. After the war the larger issues of Confederacy versus Union atrophied. Marauders rode roughshod over the countrysides, as in flat Kansas, burning, plundering and killing, former soldiers from both sides formed bands of what during the war had been termed guerillas, after the war these bloody bands, with no prospects during peace and who had been four years raiding and plundering, came together to continue their wartime ferocity.

During the war these misfits had been held together by a very tenuous idealism, afterwards they rode together for plunder, nothing more, nothing less.

They were the successors of the fighting Indians. In time they would go the way of the Indians, but it would be a while yet, and although their wild raids had originally been confined to the devastated Southern states, they inevitably widened the scope of their raids into sparsely settled areas such as west Texas, the New Mexico Territory which included what many years later would include the State of Arizona. They also raided northward.

They arrived suddenly, usually shortly before dawn, killed and burned and were gone before afternoon. They were elusive as smoke; experienced, shrewd, led by bloodthirsty renegades whose wartime experience made them perfectly capable of striking even fair-sized towns. Isolated cow outfits taken by surprise had no chance, not even large outfits with perhaps a dozen riders.

Marauders rode in bands of as many as thirty to forty renegades. Losses were sustained, but for every dead renegade two or three more rode in and joined up.

Spartanville hadn't even heard of raiders in its part of central Colorado. Indians, yes, outlaws, of course, but the only stories they heard of marauders trickled in by way of stage drivers or travelers and they almost invariably were about events that had happened hundreds of miles southward, either in the border country or perhaps back east somewhere.

The first hint of trouble arrived with the driver of one of Old Man Bulow's rattle-trap stages. A place called Cortez far south near the New Mexico–Colorado line had been attacked before sunrise when folks were still abed by a band of outlaws who had killed a dozen people and had set the town afire.

Gerald Shoup passed the driver's tale off with a flourish of his wiping rag. 'Messicans,' he opined. 'Hell, they're always raidin' down over the line

13

an' up into New Messico. If it isn't a revolution it's outlaw *bandoleros*, a mixture of Apaches, Messicans, white killer-scum.'

From experience the people of the higher plains and mountain country had been listening to stories of Mexico's internal wars, revolutions, uprisings, raidings and murders since Hector was a pup. They just naturally accepted the stageman's story and passed it along with a few nods of the head and little comment.

Dave Petrie was overhauling a Winchester saddlegun some cowman had used as a crowbar when he heard the tale. Like everyone else, he believed what he heard and let it pass in favor of replacing the cowman's warped gun barrel.

It was a pleasant springtime day. There were honey bees among the flowers, particularly the hyacinth and flourishing stands of overpoweringly scented lilac. Spartanville went about its normal activities, the blacksmith worked metal over his anvil, two horsing mares at the liveryman's corral were squealing at each other, three boys were driving a warped old buggy tire along with shouts when the rim wouldn't go straight, and women in bonnets carrying mesh bags entered and left the general store.

The nearest thing to something unusual was the appearance of three dirty, slovenly, heavily-armed strangers who entered town from the north, tied up out front of Gerald Shoup's place and went inside where they remained for the better part of an hour, genial, unhurried, talkative, the kind of strangers Gerald liked. Gerald was quite a talker too.

They left town riding south. Dave saw them, paid no particular attention and went down to the general store for some light machine oil along with a box of thirty-thirty ammunition he would need when he tested the new barrel in the cowman's saddlegun.

The liveryman had a large brindle dog. When those three strangers were nearing the end of town the dog went to the front of the barn and growled. He did not bark, he watched the horsemen pass and growled. They paid no attention to him.

In mid-afternoon several cowmen appeared in town. It was getting along toward the time of year for rounding up and trail-driving to railhead where there was almost an acre of lodgepole pine shipping corrals.

Old Man Bulow, whose first name was Ambrose, drifted over to the saloon along toward evening. He'd been a widower for close to twenty years and like most old widowers, was indifferent about personal appearance. He didn't visit the barber until he absolutely had to, he wore the same ancient hat he'd worn for thirty years and although he washed his shirts in a corralyard trough, he did not own a flat iron. Also, when he lost a button he did not replace it although years earlier he had sewn buttons back on. Now, his excuse was valid, he couldn't thread a needle worth a damn.

2
Big Odds

They didn't come in a wild, noisy rush with guns blazing and the sun still below the horizon. If they had Spartanville would eventually have recovered and fought back. Instead, they came like coyotes, without a sound, three were inside the bank, two more were at the corralyard standing over Old Man Bulow's iron bed in the harness room with drawn pistols.

The leader, an unshaven, lean and weathered man who could have been in his fifties but who acted more like twenty-five, was sitting comfortably inside the general store when the clerk came to open up just shy of sunrise. He smiled broadly without raising the six-gun in his lap. He made a little gesture with his free hand. 'Come in, lad. Now then—close the door.'

The clerk, too young to understand, obeyed every order to the letter. He expected the storekeeper to be along directly. For years his custom had been to have an early breakfast at the cafe then come directly to the store which would be open for business with the clerk feather-dusting shelves and counters.

At the bank in its proud building of red brick, the routine was about the same; the chief cashier, a beanpole addicted to eye shades and brocaded vests, opened the iron shutters, unlocked the roadway door, opened the safe to put money in his cash drawer for the day's business, then puttered until the banker arrived.

Outwardly nothing had changed in Spartanville but just before the sun came over the distant curve of the world someone fired a six-gun; but even that might not have alarmed the town, varmints raiding trash barrels were common. They also raided chicken roosts, storehouses if they could gnaw through.

Just that one shot, the signal the raiders had been awaiting. At the bank where James Westphal was rigidly immobilized by shock when his chief cashier was struck down from behind by a russet-bearded man with a flour sack in his free hand which held the contents of the vault.

The bullet from that one shot struck the store-keeper dead center. He might have been punched backwards if he hadn't been a very heavy man. He simply dropped his jaw, popped his eyes wide and collapsed. His clerk had turned to stone in front of a counter of bolt goods.

The lean, weather-darkened man arose smiling, turned and shot the clerk. Later, there was an argument among townsmen that lasted for years. After those first two shots it had sounded like a war. Some said there had been eighteen shots, others said more like ten, maybe twelve. At the time none of this was important because after the flurry of gunshots folks tumbling out of beds heard running horses, and that was another sore point. Some swore those horses fled northward. Folks nearer the lower end of town like the blacksmith swore they went south.

The truth was simply that they had split up, half going north, half going south.

For Dave Petrie the shock came slowly as Old Man Bulow was hauled out of his harness room by the heels with a little puckered red hole in the center of his forehead. Ambrose Bulow may have been slovenly, careless where he expectorated his cud juice, but he possessed a lot of rough virtues; he didn't deserve being killed in his sleep. Neither did the storekeeper and his clerk, neither did James Westphal at the bank who, to some folks anyway, had curdled milk of human kindness, but being shot point-blank, unarmed and surprised, standing there in the bank doorway wide-eyed and rigid when he was deliberately murdered—he deserved better.

For once the cafeman did almost no early-morning business. Townsmen went around looking for the dead. There was a muttered consensus that Spartanville had been hit by marauders but for a while this notion was not unanimous. Raiders, folks knew, did not come sneaking in the night, they came hell-for-leather, guns blazing.

Gerald Shoup, without his barman's apron, took

a jolt of his own whiskey and Gerald was not a drinking man. There were widows and orphans now too, there were brains and blood on walls, and whether or not it had been an orthodox raid it sure as hell had been one.

Dave Petrie took Gerald and a few other men on the ensuing manhunt. One of his companions protested in exasperation when Dave led off northward. He knew for a blessed fact they had gone south. He lived near the lower end of town; he'd heard riders running past just about sunrise.

The gunsmith silenced this man with a frown. 'North. I was in the alley peeing. I heard the gunshots and saw a band of raiders . . . Look there, right up the damned stageroad north as straight as an arrow.'

The tracks were plain in new-day brilliance. Running shod horses dig in in front and scuff dirt backwards with their rear shoes.

They were armed but Dave had a Winchester rifle sticking up out of his saddle boot, which had been made for a carbine not a rifle. He also had a six-gun in its hip-holster, old, without a shred of bluing on it, but in perfect working condition, Dave Petrie's favorite handgun.

None of them owned saddle stock; they had appropriated them from the dead liveryman's barn and corrals.

To the diminishing local opinion that it had not been an orthodox raid, it was pointed out by the true believers that except for coming like Comanches, all the rest of it was typical of marauders.

The town had been pretty well emptied of money; there were other similarities. When the manhunters eventually returned empty-handed on worn-down horses, Gerald Shoup finished off the skeptics the night of the raid with one angry statement.

'What in hell is the bickering about? Call it anythin' you want to, the town was hit by a band of hard-riders. What happened to us has been happenin' in other places for years. Maybe we been lucky, bein' so far north, but our luck run out an' no matter what you call it, we was attacked an' hit hard by a band of renegades!'

Dave Petrie rode out the next morning alone. The victims of the raid were cleaned up in town, solemnly loaded on to a flatbed wagon and driven out to the graveyard. Mourners followed the wagon. The entire town turned out. If anyone missed the gunsmith it was not mentioned.

Dave Petrie did not expect to be missed. There were too many corpses, too much shock. The dead constituted some of the most respected men in Spartanville.

All shot dead at one time, in the space of maybe fifteen or twenty minutes without any warning, something completely unexpected. It was devastating.

The gunsmith made good time. Until he reached the place where his companions had turned back last night, no longer able to read sign, he did not have to follow tracks. After he got up where they had turned back, he rode slower.

The land began changing as it got closer to a low, spiney-ridged set of foothills, heavily timbered, after which there was a long, very narrow valley which ran for miles beyond where the genuine mountains arose.

The tracks would have been more difficult to follow if it had been a single rider or maybe a pair of riders. The marks he traced out had been made by what he thought could have been six or eight riders. It could have even been ten riders; after the tracks left the roadway they tended northwesterly. The grass was flourishing, it bruised easily. Dave tried to guess where the tracks would end. He was squinting in all directions. Somewhere there had to be either a camp or at least a resting place; horses, particularly horses that had been ridden hard, had to be rested or they gave out.

He was squinting in the direction of the tracks across open country with only an occasional tree and a wide scattering of large rocks, when his horse missed a lead and swung its head northward, ears up.

The horseman was backgrounded in an open vale by sunshine and rank after rank of large old trees. He was sitting motionless watching the gunsmith.

Dave did not stop nor more than glance north-ward, but the hair on the back of his neck arose. He continued northwesterly until he could only see the man watching him by twisting in the saddle, which he did not do.

The horse dipped into a low, wide swale. Dave doubted that the watcher could see him while he was down in there, so he halted, stepped off, went back to the easterly slope and wormed his way up until he could see the horseman.

He was not there.

Dave scanned the area, there was no sign of the watcher, no movement, no sound of shod horse-shoes over stone.

The hair on his neck was still stiff. He crawled back until he could stand up, went to his horse and turned northward, kept out of sight in the arroyo until he could see ahead where the shallow place was rising toward a headland of huge trees.

He had two choices; hope he would not be seen in the arroyo, hope he could get into the yonder trees before the watcher guessed he had been in the arroyo, or turn back, follow the arroyo's south-ward course in the direction of town.

He considered the position of the sun; he still had about five or six hours of daylight, maybe a tad more; this time of year days got gradually longer.

If the watcher had been one of the marauders there would be others, possibly in camp some-where in the timber or maybe even as far ahead as that long, narrow strip of land between the foothills and the mountains.

Sure as hell if the watcher belonged to the raiders he wouldn't waste time finding the others and warning them they were being tracked, and that meant, if the killers decided to find the lone tracker, Dave had something like six or eight enemies to deal with.

He needed darkness—or a miracle—neither of which seemed likely to arrive in time regardless of which course he chose.

He turned back southward. There was no way to ascertain whether that watcher would rouse his friends and come after the gunsmith. There was an excellent chance they wouldn't. If they were resting they might not. If their animals were rested there was a fair chance they would, if for no other reason to leave the gunsmith's riddled corpse as a warning to anyone else from Spartanville who might feel brave.

He did not ride hastily. There were many things a four-year veteran of war learned that were useless to him in peacetime, unless he had ridden with cavalrymen whose survival depended exclusively on ruse, subterfuge, slyness and horseflesh.

There was one thing Confederate cavalrymen had excelled in; night-riding surprise attacks and the art of ambush.

Dave Petrie had learned these lessons well, otherwise he would not have been in the arroyo, he would have been somewhere between the capitals of two enemy nations in an unmarked grave.

If he had much of an advantage it was in the fact that he knew the territory as well as anyone and better than most. He had at one time or another, either as a pot-hunter or simply as a curious rider, visited every part of it for a hundred miles in all directions.

The arroyo did not run straight south. Arroyos, formed over the centuries by torrential rains, made brawling waterways which cut their own paths in mostly a mindless and erratic pattern.

This one was no different. What it lacked was tree-cover. For the gunsmith's purpose it possessed something better, huge boulders massive waves of water had tumbled and rolled for miles.

He followed around a bend, dismounted and crawled near the top of a grassy topout. For almost a quarter of an hour, with hope rising that they would not be back there, he lay lizard-like. Behind him down in the arroyo it was so still and quiet he could hear his horse cropping grass.

Then he saw them, slouching along as they followed his shod-horse sign. Six of them, riding like Indians, one behind the other even in places where the arroyo was wide enough for them to couple up.

He squinted at the sun. The afternoon was slipping away so gradually it seemed the sun was not moving at all.

He went back, mounted and continued without

haste for almost a mile where a huge stone was embedded in one side of the arroyo. There were three trees behind it. Where the trail would pass, it was confined because of the obtrusive big rock. In this choke-point the men following him would have to ride single file.

Dave went as far as the huge boulder, hobbled the horse so that between the mammoth rock and the trees the horse would not be visible until the riders got past and could look back.

He did not smile as he made his preparations but he might have; this was what those old craggy Secesh had taught him. Have a clear field of fire in front and a way for a swift withdrawal behind. Always figure you're going to be out-numbered; never put your back where you can't get away very quickly without having to overcome obstacles such as forests, rivers, stone fences and soggy ground.

He put his six-gun beside himself close at hand, found a niche where his rifle fitted, settled down to wait with rifle hammer at full cock and eventually heard a complaining, nasal voice say, 'Len, he ain't important for chris'sake. We should be goin' north not back down near that town again.'

For a long moment as the men rode closer to the dog-leg beyond which was the mighty boulder there was no answer, then it came in a fierce tone of voice.

'We never set back an' let damned fools try to

make trouble. We'll find him when this arroyo peters out an' he's got to ride in open country.'

The complainer replied in the same whining voice. 'Catch the subbitch—for what? Maybe he ain't even from that town. Maybe he's some feller out for meat, or maybe . . .'

'Shut—up!' the other man said. 'We're goin' to teach them folks not to send out spies. We'll do like we done with others. Prop him up so's they'll find him.'

Dave eased his head down. The first man who came around the dog-leg was going to hell in a hand cart. But they stopped just before moving past the dog-leg. There was a little conversation, too quietly spoken for Dave to distinguish individual words. The hair on the back of his neck was straight up.

If they had in some way guessed what lay ahead, dismounted and scattered, Dave would never leave this place alive. He had cold sweat running when a deep, bull-voice spoke on the far side of the dog-leg. 'Len, that's brandy. I don't like brandy. It burns and . . . I told you we should have raided the saloon. This stuff ain't fitten for man or beast.'

Len's reply was as short with this raider as it had been with the other complainer. 'You got money. Next town we find you can do the spyin'-out, an' buy your own damned liquor. Let's go, this arroyo's got to peter out not very far ahead.'

Dave raised a limp cuff to mop off sweat,

hunched lower when the first rider appeared passing through the dog-leg of the arroyo.

The first complainer spoke again. 'Crazy. We should be thirty miles through them mountains an' . . .'

The sound of the gunshot created panic in their horses. Each renegade had to concentrate on controlling a terrified animal.

Dave levered up, crouched and fired again. The first kill was the outlaw with the nasal voice. He had been speaking when the bullet knocked him off his horse. Where he landed dust lifted.

The second man Dave hit was squaw-reining his horse as though the bit was a wood-saw. It did not settle the frightened animal, it made him fight harder. He bogged his head and bucked straight into two other riders, past them and directly toward the gunsmith's huge rock.

This shot Dave could not have missed with a blindfold. The second outlaw threw up his hands. The horse did the rest, it bucked him off so hard he flew over its head. He did nothing to break the fall. He too was dead.

Pandemonium filled the arroyo. Men shouted, at least two or them fired handguns at the big rock. They made splinters fly.

Dave ducked. Sharp stone splinters could cause serious injury. As he came up slowly there was no visible movement, the renegades had raced back around the dog-leg.

Two men, both face down, arms flung wide, were what remained. Dave cocked his head. The renegades were riding hard back the way they had come. When the gunsmith was sure they would not return, soon anyway, he went down, emptied the pockets of the corpses, flung their weapons as far as he could, went behind the trees, removed the hobbles, got astride and set his course for town. Shadows were already appearing on the east side of trees, buildings, and big ambush-rocks.

He rode twisted until the rooftops and roadways of Spartanville came out of the late afternoon to him. There was no pursuit, nor had he expected there to be.

It was dusk by the time he had cared for the horse, walked into his shop, lighted a coal oil lamp and emptied his pockets atop his work bench.

Each dead man had the same amount of green-backs in his pockets. Wherever their camp had been they had used the time dividing the loot from Westphal's bank and the general store.

There wasn't much else of interest, clasp knives, some silver coins, odds and ends and one letter addressed to a man named Boyd. The first name was illegible. Most of the contents were also illegible. The man who owned the letter had been carrying it in a pocket for three years. If, whoever Boyd had been he had not answered that letter in three years, for a fact he would never answer it.

Dave locked the shop, went down to the cafe, ate

like a horse then went up to the saloon where Gerald cocked an eye as he said, 'Where'n hell you been?'

The gunsmith waited until his drink was brought, then leaned down atop the counter and told the story from beginning to end. Before he finished there was not a sound in the saloon. Townsmen and a scattering of outlying stockmen seemed to be welded in place.

3

A Long Ride

Gerald broke the stunned silence speaking dryly. 'Well; I expect the vigilantes better be called up; sure as hell's hot them bastards aren't goin' to have two of their friends shot . . . An' there's somethin' else: Dave saw six of 'em. That'd be the bunch that run north . . . Now then, when they all come together again . . .' The saloonman paused looking at his silent customers. 'How many of them will there be?'

The solemn customers along Shoup's bar and among the poker tables stared at Dave Petrie. An old cowman threw down a handful of cards and arose with a sizzling curse. 'Petrie . . . Now I got to get home. You stirred up a nest of rattlers. Maybe they'll just get revenge on the town, but I'm not goin' to bet on it that they won't raid out-lying cow outfits.'

After the stockman departed Shoup and his

remaining patrons continued to regard the gunsmith from closed faces. Dave had a defense but did not mention it except to say the odds out yonder had been six to one, then he returned to his shop and bedded down, unable to sleep until along toward dawn.

The gunsmith's action probably could have been avoided. There was a fair chance he could have fled all the way back to town and safety. The difficulty with something like this was simply if he *had not* been able to reach Spartanville, he would have ended up propped against a tree beside the road somewhere as full of holes as a sieve.

Spartanville became alert and watchful. Only a few folks would speak to Dave Petrie. People who turned immediately to guns for solutions invariably became victims of retaliation which did not necessarily involve weapons. Not at first anyway.

What happened after the two killings was a kind of retaliation folks might have expected. The first attack which had resulted in four murders had been slyly and cleverly secretive. Retaliation came to Spartanville the same way, but this time it put a cold chill in the heart of everyone.

Four days after the gunsmith's shoot-out in the arroyo, Spartanville awakened to a horrible surprise. Four local women were missing. No notes had been left behind, nothing else was missing, no horses or weapons, and certainly no money, just four women, two unmarried sisters of the defunct banker, spinster ladies, and the daughter of the blacksmith, a woman in her early twenties, and a much younger girl; fourteen-year-old Pearl Tweedy, daughter of the widow-woman who owned and operated the rooming house.

Only one person came forward to give information: Lily Tweedy, weathered, thin-lipped, cranky as a bitch wolf. She told folks she had heard something that could have been a muffled outcry in her daughter's bedroom. It hadn't been repeated, nevertheless fiercely-protective Lily Tweedy had gone to see. Her daughter was not in bed. Lily assumed she was out back in the outhouse and returned to bed. In the morning she discovered the wide-open window through which her daughter had been taken, and below the window boot tracks.

It required no great power of perception to understand what had happened, and the few folks who had continued to nod to the gunsmith, no longer did so. In fact there was a murmur about lynching him. It had started with the burly, no-nonsense blacksmith, a powerful man in his prime with enough hair on his lower face to make up for what he lacked on top. His name was Jack Gibbons. His smithy was at the lower end of town opposite Old Man Bulow's corralyard, which had been taken over by his nephew who had been a range rider, and was capable, tough as a boiled owl, and, so it was said, short-tempered, a man about thirty-five named Jed Bulow.

Jed and the blacksmith harangued for a lynching. Although there was resentment against the gunsmith, folks were not ready to lynch him. The argument in his favor was that in order to save his own life, and with no idea what kind of retaliation would follow, he had done what most folks would have done.

Jack Gibbons and Jed Bulow countered that argument by saying Petrie should have known those raiders wouldn't let the killing of two of their band go by without some kind of revenge.

Gerald Shoup disagreed over his bar. Speaking from experience he said, 'When a man's back's to the wall he don't think of but one thing—stayin' alive. He don't think about what could be a result of defendin' himself.'

This bias never entirely died, but for most folks, like the issue of Shoup's saloon being across from the church, something occurred to take its place.

Two days after the abductions a southbound stage entered Spartanville from the nearest town up-country, a place called Bridger's Crossing.

It had been stopped midway by a band of horsemen led by a weathered, hawk-faced man who had a gold toothpick in his mouth when he rode up beside the near-side of the rig ignoring frightened passengers to hand the driver a piece of paper. Not a word passed between them. The riders on the west side of the road sat like statues. Ten of them.

The weathered-darkened man reined away and gestured for the whip to be on his way.

The whip handed the scrap of paper to Jed Bulow, explained where and how he had got it, then went up to Shoup's saloon with his story, and as he was holding everyone's attention with his recitation, Gerald placed a full-to-the-brim shot glass of corn whiskey in front of him, then stood waiting and watching.

The whip, an older man with scars to prove he was not easily shaken, lifted the glass, held it briefly poised then dropped its contents down without so much as a sigh. His hand had been as steady as stone.

Having passed his test of manhood, the whip shoved the glass forward for a refill. Gerald nodded, refilled the glass which the stager did not touch as he finished his story for the saloon full of hushed listeners.

'It said unless folks handed over the son of a bitch who killed two of their companions in a bushwhack, folks wouldn't want their women back after the raiders was through with 'em.' The stager downed his second jolt with the aplomb he had demonstrated with the first before also saying, 'The note said folks had two days to bring the gun-smith in the direction of the foothills where the renegades would meet them an' take Dave Petrie away with 'em. There was to be no more'n two fellers to accompany the gunsmith.'

Someone muttered into the silence. 'Day after tomorrow,' and that made it easy for others to speak. Jed Bulow looked darkly vengeful when he spoke from the bar. 'How about this evenin'? Or first thing in the morning?'

No one spoke for a long time. Gerald went along his bar collecting empties and making wide sweeps with the bar rag he wore tucked under his apron. He looked as black as thunder.

Later, he went up to the gun shop and told Dave the story. He refrained from mentioning Jed Bulow's retort, he simply said, 'If you got a brain the size of a pea, you'll get on your horse after sundown an' never look back.'

It was sound advice.

When Dave went down to the cafe although the place had a number of other diners not a one of them so much as raised his head to acknowledge the gunsmith's presence.

Later, long after dark when there were few lights showing, the gunsmith took his long-barreled Winchester, a boot knife and an under-and-over .44 derringer, saddlebags with food in them and rode up the back alley at a dead walk heading northward.

Gerald had neglected to tell him there were eleven renegades because all the whip had said about that was that there was a lot of them where his coach had been stopped. The fact was that he had not counted them.

It turned off chilly with a scimitar moon over-head in a star-studded night. Springtime was giving way to summer, which made little differ-ence; Colorado got cold almost every night; coldest a few hours before dawn, by which time the gunsmith had passed the arroyo, riding paral-lel to it, and had got into the foothills where he rested the horse on the rim which separated that long, narrow slot from the massive bulk of the more distant and heavily timbered mountains.

He dismounted and squatted. There was no tell-tale supper fire. It had either been doused earlier, before the renegades got into their soogans, or had never been lighted. He suspected the latter; he was not seeking greenhorns.

False dawn was a long time coming. He hun-kered beside his dozing horse chewing jerky. If they made a fire now he probably would not be able to discern it, unless they used wet or half-dry wood, in which case there would be smoke.

There was no smoke for an excellent reason, the renegades used only dry wood which burned hot and fast without smoke.

Dave felt stubble on his jaw before finally deciding he was not going to locate the raiders' camp from his hunkering place.

He led his horse back downslope a short dis-tance before mounting, then got into the timber holding to a northerly course, which required constant correction because in places the forest giants were too close-spaced for a man on horseback to hold to a straight line.

Heat did not arrive, not even after the sun was climbing. Stiff treetops shut it out in all but a very few places, usually where lightning strikes had caused fires which left grassy sites usually of no more than several acres in size.

With no particular goal, he sashayed east and west. Wherever the raiders were, there would be one direction they would not go—southward. Not until the day after tomorrow, which now, with a new day at hand, would be tomorrow.

He rode toward the highest places, confident the raiders would have another watcher lower down where he could see all the range country between the highlands and the lowlands, the way a watcher had seen Dave.

A horse's sense of smell is far superior to the sense of smell of a man. Dave watched his horse's ears, but the animal trudged along concerned only with moving through and around big trees.

Nothing broke the hush except occasional scolding birds far overhead among tree tops. He came to the verge of one of those grassy clearings, this one about three or four acres in size. Four wapiti were standing out there, grass protruding from both sides of their mouths, looking intently in Dave's direction. They too had an enhanced sense of smell. Although pine and fir needles muffled the sound of his horse, the wapiti had the gunsmith's scent and stood only until they could discern his moving horse, then, with trumpeting snorts they fled.

Dave halted, swung off and stood at the head of his horse trailing one rein. The horse had been briefly interested in the large animals which disappeared across the meadow where forest giants made perpetual gloom.

Dave stood motionless with the horse. It appeared that the manhunt he had embarked upon just very well might turn out to be a lot of fruitless riding. What he needed was a sign—any kind, a broken lower limb where men had passed by, a scent strong enough to be detected by his horse, maybe even sounds of riders.

Where he stood the world was steeped in an ancient silence. Even birds did not seem to live on the edge of the clearing.

He sighed and got back astride. He did not enter the clearing, he skirted around it before beginning to angle eastward.

He had to guess about it, but thought he could be higher than the raiders would be camped. He was fairly certain of one thing; if they intended to meet townsmen tomorrow they would be camped close to the verge of foothills where they had a clear view of riders from town.

On this basis he did not go across the narrow slit of land separating the timbered foothills from the massive and higher mountains northward.

It was a good guess. It was almost a fatal one. He was peering southward as he passed silently among huge old trees when he heard a woman scream. The scream was not repeated but it had seemed close enough for him to fix its general location. He was closer to the source of that outcry than he liked; the sound had come from below the ridge southward but no farther easterly than he now was.

The horse threw up its head, perhaps at the scream, perhaps because it had caught a scent, man-scent or horse-scent.

He left his horse where shadows would hide it unless it moved; where raiders would not find it unless it nickered at the scent of other horses, took his rifle and scouted very carefully in the direction of the scream. No scolding birds appeared, which was fortunate. It was also an indication that other earthbound creatures were close.

This particular area had pines and firs growing so close together even a man on foot could not always pass between them. As cover it was ideal, as obstacles to his stalk it was a pain in the butt.

Once he thought he heard a man's gruff laughter, but that was not repeated either. He altered course only a little and slowed his stalk according to the nearness of trees.

It was cool as well as shadowy. He came across a little piddling creek, bare of the usual verge-growth because of the layers of matted, resin-impregnated fir and pine needles.

At this place he found where horses had watered. From here on he made very slow progress. When he finally halted he could make out a camp through the timber in a small clearing.

Men were loafing or eating, or cleaning and fresh-loading weapons. He counted them twice, both times coming up with the same number—eleven.

It surprised him. He had no reason to believe those raiders who had fled southward had not kept going in that direction. Obviously this is not what happened. They had circled far out and around to rendezvous with the men who had fled northward.

At the moment he did not speculate how they had found each other, he thought instead that odds of eleven to one were the equivalent to suicide and hunkered down among the trees watching as men came and went, ate and lolled around smoking. There were two empty bottles to reflect slanting sunlight.

The horses were not in sight. It was not hard to imagine that the renegades had searched out one of those little grassy clearings where their animals could graze.

He arose and backed a hundred feet before striking out uphill toward the verge again. He had counted eleven men; if there were no more, then he could cross above the camp on the verge without fear, but if there were more renegades, scouts or watchers, what he had in mind was not going to succeed without one hell of a lot of luck.

So far his luck had held, but the problem with luck is that it could change in a twinkling. Nevertheless he skulked along the top of the verge using shadows and trees the way Indians had done.

Evidently his luck had not deserted him. He was eastward a fair distance looking southward when he saw movement up ahead and slightly lower down where hobbled horses were either eating in a clearing, or standing hip-shot dozing in shade.

Thirteen horses not eleven. He worried about that until he remembered that the horses of the two men he had shot from ambush had run back up the arroyo, stirrups flapping, behind the fleeing renegades.

If he guessed wrong there might be two renegades unaccounted for, and that worry slowed his downslope approach to the clearing.

Every time he stopped to look and listen, he lost more time. The day was drawing to its end, what sunlight appeared in those clearings but nowhere else had a slanting, coppery tint.

Dave finally halted with two massive fir trees at his back and an equally as massive series of pines in front. The nearest horse, a dappled sorrel, threw up its head staring in his direction. If there was a guard out here he would see that.

Dave waited, the horse wearied of his vigil and went back to cropping feed. Every horse out there was hobbled, some with chain hobbles, some with loop-through Mormon hobbles.

He remained still as shadows deepened and darkened; as dusk came he heard men approaching and froze with his rifle in both hands.

They passed a good hundred and fifty feet farther downslope, talking as they passed. Where they halted to look at the horses one man said, 'Len should have wrote on the piece of paper he wanted all the money them folks could scrape together along with that murderin' son of a bitch.'

His companion replied tartly. 'Did you ever try to tell Len anythin'? It'd be like spittin' in the ocean expectin' to raise the water level.'

'Well, they're all right over here, let's get back an' get somethin' to eat.'

Dave watched them turn back, walking loosely without making a sound. Dusk was passing. He heard someone angrily denounce whoever had tossed a short scantling of green pine on the supper fire.

Dave waited, smelled cooking, heard men call to one another, began his slow and cautious approach toward the nearest horse. It watched him without moving. He removed the hobbles, left them lying in the grass and moved to the next horse. Only twice did he encounter spooky animals, one of them snorted and backed off. The other one hopped faster than a man could run. He left those two. In fact he left all the horses, scrambled back close to the verge above the little meadow, fired his handgun over the heads of the horses, then hurried as fast as he could back toward his own animal.

He heard the yelling as renegades went over to the clearing. There were only two horses out there, the spooky one and the horse that could hop in hobbles faster than a man could run.

4

The Unexpected

No one with the sense gawd gave a chicken would go up against a gang of killers, but he could outfox them if they did not know he was in their vicinity; he could set all but two of them afoot, which was exactly what he had schemed to do and had done.

It might not destroy them as a band but it sure-Lord would create confusion and delay. It was a delay he was counting on.

It was getting darker by the minute. In open country it might still be dusk, in the big timber it was full night as Dave set his horse to a fast walk back the way he had come.

He had seen no women at that camp, but then he hadn't dawdled a lot. They had to be there, somewhere, whether he had seen them or not he had heard that scream.

Stamping on an anthill, striking a hornets' nest with a stick, and setting renegades afoot in timbered country all had the same result, angry critters fanning in all directions seeking the cause of their disaster.

Dave dropped down-country until he thought he was about equal with that dry-camp back yonder, and this time when he swung off to hobble his animal he afterwards did not move very far. The unhorsed outlaws would want his animal quite possibly even more than they wanted him.

The forest was quiet, nocturnal critters would be abroad but for the most part they were stealthy creatures, most of them hunted by scent, it became too dark to do otherwise. What the gunsmith was straining to hear was man-noise. They would be hunting him like wolves. He had done what they had not thought possible. They would kill him on sight for setting them afoot, but their rage went deeper; he had hit them where they had been most vulnerable and had done it very effectively, something like that was as hard on their pride as the actual loss of their animals.

Somewhere distant, possibly as far as the mountains beyond that narrow long slit, a wolf made his mourning sound; he had lost his mate. It was the kind of sound that made prehistoric man stand perfectly still scarcely breathing. It did the same for modern man.

After the final echoes passed the gunsmith moved easterly a hundred yards. They were out there, somewhere. Most of them would have gone after their horses but not all of them.

It was a long wait with darkness beginning to turn cold before he heard a careless individual coursing up and down from north to south, so full of rage he was not as cautious as he should have been. Still, the noise of his downhill approach as he completed one of his north to south sweeps, was audible only providing someone was waiting to hear it.

Dave gauged the soft sound of boots treading pine and fir needles to place where the man would pass on his southward sweep.

It would be a fair distance east of where he was waiting. Easy rifle distance but too dark to get good aim. He began a totally silent stalk to effect a closer sighting when the renegade passed along. Unlike the furious killer, Dave had every reason to not make a sound. The odds were still eleven to one.

Someone, either Dave or his two-legged companion in this isolated place of darkness, was too close to a den which disturbed the bear whose den was not visible.

The growl was deep-throated enough to belong to a full grown bear. Dave froze with a pumping heart. Although a bear had poor eyesight, he had an incredibly keen sense of smell, and clumsy as a bear appeared, no man living could outrun one.

In a matter of moments the initiative had passed from the men to the bear. Dave no longer heard the renegade moving.

The growling stopped and that made Dave particularly uneasy. Bears were not normally nor traditionally nocturnal creatures, but each bear marked its territory and was belligerent toward trespassers night or day.

Silence settled. Even small nocturnal animals had either gone to ground or were tensely motionless. Dave picked up a rock and hurled it. The bear growled again. This time the sound came from a different direction; the bear was out of its den, darkness or no darkness. If it had cubs, which was possible although early spring was well past so they would no longer be babies, the bear was doubly dangerous. There was nothing on earth more deadly than a sow bear with cubs.

The growling now was northward. If the critter was tracking by scent it was going uphill, not downhill where Dave was frozen in place.

He heard the man yell, heard him lever up and fire his Winchester three times in succession. He also heard the bear roar and moments later the man screamed.

Dave went toward the sounds in a quick trot. He had an advantage; the bear was after the renegade, her back was to the gunsmith.

He had no difficulty locating them, the bear had knocked the man down. He had lost his gun and was trying to scramble to his feet. Each time he got part way up, the bear swung a huge paw and sent the man sprawling.

They made enough noise to attract attention for many yards. The man did not yell again but

Dave had one quick look at his face, it was bloody and contorted with fear.

The bear backed off for a moment or two, customary bear behavior during an attack.

Dave sank to one knee, took long aim and fired. The bear had been hit in one of its rare areas which produced instant death, behind the ear and several inches to the left. Bears were normally not easy to kill, especially if they were aroused, but this one did not even try to twist to see who was behind it. It simply fell in a big shaggy heap.

The gunshot echo did not travel far among the trees. Dave walked over, kicked the renegade's carbine away, yanked the man's six-gun away and flung it among the trees, he then used one hand to hoist the man to his feet. He was tall and wide with a rawboned build and he smelled. Dave led him to a tree, pushed him down with his back to rough bark and wrinkled his nose. No wonder the bear had gone after him instead of Dave.

The man was bloody and badly shaken, he looked at the gunsmith from a bloody face numb with shock. Dave leaned aside the rifle, knelt and tied off the man's worst wounds, then settled back on his heels returning the big man's dumb stare as he spoke. 'You're lucky that old bear wasn't a sow with cubs. She wouldn't have set back, she would have torn you to pieces.'

The renegade's tongue made a swift, furtive circuit of his lips. He had four bloody rakers on the left side of his face. Dave handed the man his bandana, told him to hold it tightly over the claw gouges, waited until the man did this, then said, 'You got a name?'

'Ames Boyd.'

'Can you think of a good reason why I shouldn't finish what that bear started?'

'Who—are you?'

'The feller who set you afoot. The feller who killed your two friends in that arroyo. Name's Dave Petrie. I'm the gunsmith down in Spartanville.'

The outlaw eased up the bandana, bleeding started immediately. He clamped the bandana back tightly and turned his attention to the dead bear. 'That son of a bitch come out of nowhere. I was lookin' behind me.'

Dave settled more comfortably on the needles. The wounded man hadn't been near a creek in a long time. Also, his clothing was filthy. He could have been anywhere between twenty and fifty, even in good light.

His attention went to the carbine Dave had kicked away. It was lying at the base of a huge old tree. Dave said, 'Mister, I'd as soon shoot you as look at you. Who's the head In'ian of your raider band?'

'Leonard Bowie.'

'Which way did he go?'

'I don't know. Southward I expect. That's the direction them horses went. Downhill.' The rene-

47

gade returned his gaze to the gunsmith. 'You'll never get clear,' he said. 'They're all around here lookin' for you.'

The renegade's clothing was torn. He had cuts and scratches, mostly on his upper body. The worst were the gouge marks on his face where the bear had caught him head-on. He was not only dirty, bloody and ragged, he was also slow in recovering. He talked to the gunsmith without reservation, something he would not have done otherwise. If he felt gratitude, Dave would not have believed it was sincere and he would have been correct.

He felt very little pity for the man. He brought the outlaw's attention back when he said, 'Where are the women?'

'I don't know where they are now, but we had 'em tied back in the trees.'

'Why did one of them scream?'

The renegade cautiously eased up the bandana again. Bleeding started at once, not as it had before but still too much.

Dave growled at him. 'Leave the damned thing alone. Why did that woman scream?'

The answer indicated how the renegade felt about women. 'Charley Booth went over among them in the trees. He'd taken a shine to that young girl. When he touched the girl one of the women screamed. Len called him back. I don't know why, other times Len didn't care . . . Maybe he wanted the girl for himself.'

The cold was increasing. Dave guessed it was along toward the wee hours. He sat silently figuring what he would do with his prisoner. He hadn't thought he would see any of the raiders alive.

Boyd made a suggestion as though he had read the gunsmith's mind. 'You know this country?'

'Yes. For a long distance in all directions. Why?'

'There's a ranch southwest a few miles. Out from the foothills. I can make it about that far. If you figured to take me back to that town, I'd never make it.'

'Why should I take you anywhere?'

'You want them women back? I'll make a fair hostage for you to trade with.'

Dave snorted and got to his feet. His look at the injured man was bleak. 'They wouldn't trade you for a yeller dog. Get up!'

The outlaw arose with the aid of the tree at his back. He was bruised all over. Dave retrieved his rifle and jerked his head. 'Walk. I'll steer you from behind.'

'I can't do it,' the outlaw whined, but he found the strength after the gunsmith pushed his rifle barrel into the other man's middle and cocked it.

Boyd couldn't walk very well, especially when Dave prodded him uphill in the direction of his hobbled horse. They had to stop so often Dave's patience gave out. The last time they resumed the hike he told Boyd he would kill him if he stopped again.

From some hidden pool of reserve the outlaw not only continued to walk, he also walked better, he did not stumble or sag from weariness and pain. For one thing he knew the man with the rifle had killed two of his friends. He also knew from the gunsmith's attitude and mood he hadn't been bluffing, but by the time they reached the horse, Ames Boyd was near to collapse. He sank to the ground. The bandana against his cheek was soaked. His other injuries still bled, not much but enough.

Dave removed the hobbles, up-ended his rifle to slip it into the boot, snugged up the cinch then turned leaning on his saddle as he regarded his prisoner. 'You're goin' to slow me down an' make problems,' he told the man on the ground. When Dave drew his six-gun and aimed it, the renegade spoke swiftly. 'Listen; they'll hear the gunshot, an' besides I'm worth more to you alive.'

'How are you worth anything to me?'

'I know where we got three caches. Stuff we couldn't carry; jewelry, some gold bars from a couple of banks, some little sacks of gold.'

Dave cocked the gun. 'You're a lyin' worthless son of a bitch. Stand up!'

The outlaw arose. His lips were straining against his teeth as he waited for the bullet.

Dave eased the dog down, leathered the six-gun, swung across leather and kicked his foot free of the left stirrup as he also extended his hand and arm. He had to almost literally haul the larger, weaker man behind the cantle. As he was reining away he removed the Colt from its hip-holster and shoved it into his waistband in front.

They went westerly for about two miles before the gunsmith changed course on a downhill southerly route. He did not say a word. Not even when the injured man groaned at the uneven, jolting gait of the horse.

There was a very faint sickly streak of grey along the eastern horizon before they left the foothills. It was still difficult to see for any great distance, which suited Dave fine. He rode in the direction of Spartanville.

When they got there the sun was rising. It was still chilly. His prisoner was slumped against the gunsmith's back. Now and then he made a groan.

Dave rode down the alley to the rear of the unused jailhouse, pushed and pulled his prisoner inside, locked him in a cell, locked both front and rear doors and entered the cafe looking like the wrath of gawd. The cafeman and a few diners stared. Dave had blood on his front and back, he was sunken-eyed and dog tired. He growled at the cafeman, ignored the questions fired at him until he had eaten like a horse and had drunk three cups of coffee strong enough to float horseshoes, then, as he arose to pay for his meal, he jerked his head. 'There's one of 'em locked in the jailhouse. He's not in very good shape,' and walked out of the cafe.

Up at his shop the gunsmith went to his back room, sat on the edge of the bed to rid swollen feet of his boots, peeled off the blood-stained shirt and britches and lay back.

News traveled fast in small towns. Spartanville was no exception. By the time townsmen came to knock on the gun shop door, Dave was awake but still tired. He ignored even the most insistent knocking. They blamed him for the trouble the town was in, let them knock until they were blue in the face.

Getting into the jailhouse posed only a temporary problem. The last constable, a wise lawman, had left one key to the front door with Gerald Shoup. But that only got them into the musty front office. There was only one key to the four strap-steel cages which served as cells, and Dave Petrie had it in his pocket.

The banging on the door slackened for an hour or so before it resumed, louder and more insistent than ever. Dave had made coffee, was sitting sprawled behind his counter enjoying the coffee laced with whiskey that was doing more for his body than straight whiskey would have done.

For a while he let them bang on the door before going to open it. The foremost knocker was the preacher, John Kent, clustered behind him were the blacksmith, Gerald Shoup and three other townsmen. They would have pushed inside but Dave did not move away from the door. He glowered at them. 'Well; did you talk to the prisoner?'

The blacksmith answered. 'He's out of his head. What did you do to him an' where's the women?'

'I didn't do anything to the son of a bitch, a bear did. It would have mauled him to death if I hadn't shot it . . . If I'd used my head I'd have let the bear finish what he started—an' I don't know where the women are but I'd guess they got 'em tied to trees somewhere.'

The minister said, 'Where are they?'

Dave smiled at them without a shred of humor. 'Somewhere in the foothills scattered like quail, ten or eleven of them. I turned their horses loose.' He started to close the door. The blacksmith put a big booted foot in the way, and pushed the door wide open. 'Loose up there? You set their horses loose? You know what men like that'll do now? They'll take it out on the women.'

Dave looked steadily at the blacksmith. 'It's up to you. I've done all I can do for a while.' He kicked the big man's foot clear and slammed the door. The blacksmith swore, his companions shuffled in place with no idea what to do until Dave yelled at them through the door. 'Get a-horseback, take some rope and your guns. When I'm rested up I'll come lookin' for you . . . One more thing; don't try for prisoners, shoot 'em on sight. That's what they'll do to you.'

He returned to his chair and laced coffee behind the counter, kicked a stool around to rest his feet on, and sipped from his crockery mug.

They still blamed him. Now more than ever. Maybe he could have done more but not with a prisoner, and anyway he was worn out to the bone. That night had taken more out of him than a week of manual labor would have.

He fell asleep slouched in the chair. It was close to dusk when someone banged on the door. This time it was just one townsman. When Dave opened the door the fox-faced preacher was waiting.

'What you've done is cause more grief and worry than you know. They left town, seven of them, dead-set on killing. That's your fault too, firing them up that way. The Lord punishes men like you, Dave Petrie.'

Dave closed the door with the fox-faced minister still denouncing him. He called out. 'Why didn't you go with them? They'll need all the help they can get.'

A predictable answer came back. 'Vengeance is mine saith the Lord, I will repay.'

A disgusted gunsmith answered waspishly. 'While folks are waitin' for Him to repay those women can get pretty badly used up—you weasel-faced damned windbag. . . . Do you own a horse?'

'Yes. What of it?'

'Get him, saddle up an' meet me back here in fifteen minutes . . . Do you own a rifle?'

'No. Only a shotgun for varmints.'

'Bring that with you too . . . Fifteen minutes, you Bible-bangin' screwt.'

5

Going Back

Dave looked disreputable when he and the preacher rode up the north stage road out of town with the fox-faced man asking questions and looking apprehensive.

He got no answers until they were within a few miles of the foothills, following tracks of townsmen riding hard over the same tracks the raiders used. Then all he said was: 'Preacher, with luck you just might be the Lord's tool to repay with a vengeance.'

John Kent stared first at the gunsmith then at the nearing jumble of rocks, big trees and flinty ground rising northward, then he reined to a dead stop. 'Is that country up ahead where those raiders was camped?' he asked, and got a short answer.

'Sure is, Preacher. Get that horse moving.'

Kent did not move. 'Do you think I'm going up in there with you?'

Dave halted and sat twisted in the saddle as he smiled. 'I think you'n them other gents with big mouths blame me for what's happened, and sat on your butts in town while you did that, so now the other gents are up in here somewhere an' you're goin' up in there too, or you're goin' to stay here face down.'

They stared at each other. Kent had seen Ames Boyd back in town. He had heard rumors about someone killing two men in an arroyo northwest of town. The rumors had whispered it around that the gunsmith had killed them.

John Kent was not a coward, neither was he a fool. He gigged his horse. As they were moving again he considered the double barreled shotgun hanging awkwardly from the horn of his saddle and wagged his head.

Dave saw him do that and also considered the scattergun. 'Are you a good Christian?' he asked and got an indignant glare instead of an answer. Dave gestured toward the shotgun. 'That's your varmint gun, Preacher?'

'Yes. Raccoons, wood rats, now an' then a coyote.'

'I was told as a kid a good Christian did not believe in killin'.'

Kent's glare did not diminish. 'That don't include varmints in the chicken house nor wood rats and other pests.'

Dave slouched along eyeing the tracks ahead. There was no sign of the town posse-riders. Neither was there any indication the renegades were still up in here. He did not look at Preacher Kent when he said, 'All God's creatures got souls, Mister Kent?'

Kent got red-faced and also turned his attention to the foothills, which were close now. 'No. Not all. Human beings have souls, varmints don't.'

'How about In'ians; they got souls?'

This time the preacher flared up. 'If you want to make church-talk, come to the rectory some evenin'. Right now I don't like what we're doin' nor that timbered country up ahead which is as good bushwhackin' country as I've ever seen.'

Dave allowed the topic to die as he shifted in the saddle, leaned to consider the clear tracks underfoot, then to range a long, sweeping study of the timbered, rocky slope they were approaching.

He had set the raiders afoot last night in early dark. It was now morning of the following day. Except for the pair of horses he had not set free, there was no way for the marauders to retrieve the animals they had lost, but being *coyote* enough to out-coyote a genuine coyote, particularly under the leadership of a man who had clearly been a successful outlaw for many years, where Dave drew rein in plain sight of the yonder timber, leaned with both palms on the saddlehorn squinting from the townsmen's tracks to the tiers of yonder trees, he began to suspect that the town-riders were not going to find either the renegades or the women.

He dismounted to stand beside his horse looking up yonder and listening. There was no movement and no sound. Those town-riders'd had plenty of time to locate that raider camp—and the women. Enough time for that and to also be coming back down to open country in triumph.

Except that they were not coming; there was not a sound except for a few birds in the tree-verge watching Dave and his companion and scolding them.

Kent said, 'They've been ambushed as sure as I'm a foot tall.'

Dave glanced across the seat of his saddle, offered no reply and resumed his consideration of the rough country ahead. 'How many fellers rode out of town?' he asked.

'Seven. It would have been eight with me, except that they understood a man of the cloth couldn't go along and do what they figured to do.'

Dave commented without discontinuing his study of the rough foothill country. 'Yes indeed. But he can kill coyotes an' In'ians. . . .'

'I never killed an In'ian!'

'They was gone when you got out here, Preacher. They was varmints; ask anyone, an' varmints don't have souls.' Dave finally turned again. He was sourly smiling. 'Let's go,' he said and swung across leather.

John Kent did not move. 'You're ridin' straight down someone's rifle barrel.' He gestured. 'They can be lyin' up there like In'ians, an' most likely they are. We'll both get shot.'

Dave shook his head. 'Preacher, there's no ambush up there.'

'How can you say that?'

'Listen, Preacher. You hear the birds? Birds don't

sing from trees with men beneath them. They leave the area. Now come along.'

Reverend Kent dutifully moved out, but he rode slightly to the rear, eyes moving constantly along the gloomy inroads up ahead.

But the gunsmith did not go very far into the timber. He halted where it was cool without sunlight, studied the churned earth and sighed. 'Son of a bitch.'

John Kent scowled. 'What's the matter?'

Dave pointed earthward. 'They scattered like quail.'

Dave scowled. 'Preacher, there's seven of 'em, green as grass at manhunting. There's ten, maybe eleven raiders, every man jack of them as deadly an' sly an' wily as coyotes. If they didn't see the townsmen crossing the open country toward them . . . Preacher, those greenhorns can get grabbed one at a time like I caught Boyd, the one I brought back.'

'I didn't hear any gunfire on the ride out here,' the minister said, sounding doubtful, and Dave Petrie rolled his eyes.

'They don't have to shoot 'em. All they got to do is catch 'em one at a time, like In'ians. They don't want *them,* they want their horses. One gunshot would spoil their chances.'

Kent drifted his gaze back to the forbidding gloom up ahead as he said, 'If that's the case they'll want us for the same reason, won't they?'

Dave did not answer, he reined eastward, did not get close to the nearest foothill country, and rode steadily for almost two hours then, without a word he turned directly northward, entered the timbered area of the foothills and went up-country as straight as an arrow. Where he finally halted to give the horses a breather Kent scowled at him. 'Where are we going?'

'Try to get up near the topout where the foothills drop into a narrow long valley.'

'Two miles out of our way?'

'Yup. Men afoot wouldn't have no reason to go this far east. At least I'm prayin' they don't.'

The minister snorted. 'I'm glad you believe in the power of prayer,' he said, and followed the gunsmith when they resumed their climb among the scented pines and firs.

It was cooler where they rode through timber, but they were reminded that there was heat each time they crossed a clearing.

Dave did not look at the position of the sun but his companion did. They had not reached the northerly rim until the sun was sliding away from its meridian. To John Kent this meant they would spend the night up here, or, even if they turned back they would still be riding in darkness long before they got back to town.

Dave stopped where he could look down into that long, narrow spit of land running roughly west to east. He had heard nothing and had seen nothing, which satisfied him that, wherever the afoot out-laws were, they were not this far eastward.

He dismounted to rest his animal. Preacher Kent remained in the saddle until the gunsmith irritably said, 'A horse isn't a chair. Get down. He needs rest more than you do. *Get down!*'

The minister dismounted looking annoyed at the gunsmith's tone of voice. Spitefully he asked a question. 'All right; where are we now?'

Dave did not reply, he was gazing over treetops southward. He did not expect smoke but he hoped for dust. There wasn't any. He began to wonder if the raiders were still in the area. They could have decided to walk out of the highlands in the dark to find a ranch and horses. Unless they knew the country they would not be successful at that, especially in the night. He remembered what Ames Boyd had said about a ranch lying somewhere southwest of the foothills, and speculated that if Boyd knew where that place was, it was possible so did the others.

He had difficulty deciding whether to go to the ranch or to continue stalking through the foothills until the preacher made a remark that sounded as though he were committed to what they were doing. He said, 'We could split off a little an' sweep westerly.'

Dave looked at Kent and nodded. Westerly was the ultimate destination of that ranch; they were already in position to manhunt in that direction. He nodded, mounted and gazed dispassionately at his companion.

'Tell me something, Mister Kent, and don't get mad about the question. Was you ever an outlaw?'

The predictable reaction ensued. The fox-faced man drew himself up in the saddle. 'You got gall to ask a man a question like that. I been spreading the gospel for ten years, ploughin' an' sowing the Lord's seed.'

Dave held up his hand. 'Let's move. There isn't a lot of daylight left.'

He didn't look back, which was just as well, the preacher was glaring at his back.

They rode without haste and minimal noise. The sun continued its westerly slide, the shadows deepened among the stands of timber, they saw nothing until a bull elk with a thick neck to indicate he was in the rut, sprang out of his bed facing the riders. He had a powerful spread of antlers and he did not take a backward step.

Dave halted. The horses, unaware of danger, complacently returned the wapiti's stare. John Kent proved he had not spent all his life in churches when he very quietly said, 'Back your horse, Mister Petrie. Back him slow.'

They both backed their horses. The bull's gaze never left them. When they were far enough to avoid the charge if the bull decided to fight, Dave turned downslope into the trees. The big bull could follow their progress below him whether he could see them or not. Elk had hearing as good as that of bears. But with no sighting the big bull would not make a challenge.

Several hundred yards beyond Dave angled back to the topout. Neither of them mentioned the elk. They were entering the area where it was possible dismounted, bad tempered renegades might be, which brought the preacher to make the only remark he was to make for a long time. He said, 'Have you any idea where they're holding the women?'

Dave turned. 'You got any idea how far voices can be heard from a ridge-top?' He did not know, exactly, where the hostages had been and was not convinced, if the raiders were not in the foothills that the women wouldn't even be up in here. They were as valuable hostages as marauders could want.

A short time later the preacher did an unpreacherly thing. He unslung his scattergun, dismounted without so much as a glance at the gunsmith, left his horse standing with both reins on the ground and within moments was lost to sight.

Dave also swung down but remained with the animals. He had not seen or heard a thing, but evidently his companion had.

Dave worried about that shotgun. One blast from it would arouse every living thing, two-legged or four-legged for a radius of at least a mile.

Nothing moved that Dave could determine and there was no noise, no gunshot, no voices, nothing. He began to wonder—and worry—the fox-faced clergyman was down there somewhere among the trees in an area where a seasoned stalker would require big ears and an eye in the back of his head.

Unexpectedly when the preacher appeared he was not downslope, he was eastward along the rim they had ridden over. Dave had no time to wonder about that because John Kent was herding a filthy, unshaven, hatchet-faced individual toward Dave.

The man's holster was empty. Preacher Kent had a six-gun shoved into the front of his britches.

When the unshaven man saw Dave and the horses he stopped. John Kent growled at him. 'Go on. I'll tell you when to stop.'

Dave had the answer to the question that had most bothered him since they had entered the uplands. Whoever Kent was driving toward Dave sure as hell was one of the raiders.

'Stop,' the minister said. He then addressed the gunsmith. 'I think you was right. He's been shagging us for a while. I didn't see him but my horse kept trying to look back. Once when I turned in the saddle he was between trees. I saw him duck behind one of them.'

Dave studied the stranger. Aside from being filthy and unshaven, he was a stocky individual with the appearance of someone who lived hard. He asked the man where Leonard was and got a stone-faced answer. 'Who's Leonard?'

Behind him the minister hauled back one dog

of his scattergun, waited a moment then hauled back the other dog. The stocky man did not move but his gaze at the gunsmith wavered.

'Him an' some others went to find a ranch.'

'You didn't catch your loose horses?'

'No. A couple that wasn't turned loose is all . . . Who are you fellers?'

Dave replied gently. 'The feller behind you is Reverend John Kent from Spartanville. He told me he don't believe in killing. I'm the feller who turned your horses loose last night . . . An' caught a man named Boyd who is now in the jailhouse at Spartanville, where you'll end up, mister, if you do somethin' foolish. To tell you the truth, I'd like to put the preacher's disbelief in killin' to a test. I'd like you to do somethin' rash . . . Where are the women hostages?'

'Where they always been,' the stocky man replied. He seemed to be recovering from the shock of peering westerly where Dave and John Kent had gone, when someone pushed a shotgun against the back of his neck.

'Tied in some trees north of where you fellers got your camp?'

The captive bobbed his head without speaking. He was clearly making an assessment of his situation. Any way he considered it, he was not in a good position.

Behind him the preacher gave another order. 'Sit down!'

The prisoner sat. Kent gave another order. 'Pull up your pantlegs.' Again the prisoner obeyed, dolefully this time because he had a belly-gun in one of his boots. He did not wait to be told to throw it away, he tossed it where Dave was standing. The gunsmith picked it up and pocketed it.

Kent addressed the gunsmith. He had not raised his voice during any of this interlude and did not raise it now. 'What should we do with him?'

Before answering Dave had the man empty his pockets, and selected the only thing he wanted, a clasp knife which he also pocketed. There was a folded pad of greenbacks. Dave handed them to the minister before kneeling to use the prisoner's trouser belt to secure the man's hands behind his back and used the shell belt to tie his ankles. As he was arising he addressed the minister.

'It'd be better to cut his throat.'

The preacher was considering the stocky man when he replied. 'A headache ought to work,' and without hesitation drove the prisoner's filthy old hat down over his ears with a blow from the shotgun barrels.

Dave considered his companion. 'I'd like to ask that question again, Preacher.'

Kent gestured with his weapon toward their horses. 'We're wasting time,' he replied, went to his animal, slung the scattergun by its thong from the saddlehorn and mounted without bothering to see if the cinch was tight.

Dave got astride, looked once at the unconscious man, gave his head a slight wag and kneed his horse into moving. Someday, if he got the chance, he was going to cultivate a Bible-banger he had avoided since Kent had come into the country.

One thing was certain; preacher or not John Kent was a lot better companion on a manhunt than Dave thought, and most likely every other soul in the Spartanville country, suspected.

The sun was still up there but it was beginning to get the coppery hue from earth's dust which it got every day as it sank lower toward the saw-toothed east.

6

Friends—and Enemies

They had whittled the odds but if the gunsmith's surmise was correct there were still about eight renegades in the uplands.

He and the preacher kept to the topout for about a mile, riding carefully, particularly across rocky places where winter winds had swept the ground bare. Sound in a place like this traveled far.

That was their first disadvantage, the second one was that the farther west they rode the more the danger increased. They knew from the man they had left bound and unconscious that there were still renegades up here regardless of whether some had gone to steal horses.

And they were right; with day-long heat increasing they could have dropped lower but the gunsmith wanted as clear a view as possible, which may or may not have been wise, in any case where they crossed a particularly loose stretch of gravel and flinty chips of granite there was no way to avoid noise.

Barefoot horses would have made less noise. Shod horses scattered grit with every step.

The preacher worried about these things but his companion seemed unconcerned; he was watching the lower country for sign. Eight renegades made dust, they would also make noise.

But there was neither dust nor noise, and that worried the gunsmith. He rode light in the saddle with his belt-gun loose in leather.

They crossed a barren, gravelly spot and entered a stand of sickly pine trees. There was shade but not as much as if they had been riding a few yards downslope.

Dave's animal threw up its head with pointing ears. He stopped beside a large dead fir tree. Behind him the preacher not only reined to a halt, he also unslung his shotgun when he dismounted.

A rough voice spoke from the timber. 'Don't move!'

They were unable to see the man but his tone of voice was business-like. Dave dismounted and stood beside his horse. Behind him he thought he heard the preacher swearing under his breath.

The first man they saw was not up ahead, he came from the south and he had a cocked six-gun in his right fist. He was unshorn, unshaven, his clothing was stained and rumpled. His voice was not as menacing as the first voice had been when he told them to drop their weapons.

Another man came from behind them, also coming up the side-hill from the south. He spat tobacco juice and said nothing.

The next words came from the preacher. They rang with disgust. 'Damned fool.' They were directed at Dave Petrie but the man who had halted them from behind a dead tree wasn't sure. His retort was in the same gruff tone. 'Not as much as you are, mister. Both of you pull up your britches' leg—an' you with the shotgun, get rid of that weapon stuck in the front of your britches.'

Kent dropped the gun that had been taken from the man they had left far back. As he was doing this the two men from down the hill came closer. The one with the cocked gun eased the hammer down, leathered his weapon, ignored the captives and softly said, 'Fine lookin' animals,' to no one in particular. The other renegade ignored that remark, evidently unwilling just yet to take his attention off their captives.

The man with the gruff voice was as weather-darkened as his companions. They were fairly young, he was older with a lipless mouth and smoldering eyes. He gestured down the slope and said, 'March!'

His companions picked up the grounded weapons and followed as Dave and John Kent went down off the topout angling southward where the timber was thicker, and westerly, the direction their gruff-voiced captor ordered.

It was blessedly cool in the big timber. It was also gloomy, smelled strongly of pine and fir sap, and had slippery footing.

Not a word was said until the gruff-voiced renegade ordered his captives to halt. He stood motionless with his head cocked. Dave had heard nothing but this man thought he had, and he was right. Several men were a hundred or so yards farther down the shadowy side-hill. One of them swore as he slipped on dry needles and another voice told him to be quiet. Dave and the preacher exchanged a glance. The second voice belonged to Jack Gibbons, the blacksmith.

The older outlaw turned and half-whispered a question in Dave's direction. 'How many come up here with you?'

Dave lied with a clear conscience. 'Ten, with six or eight more followin' from town.'

The cud-chewing outlaw hissed at the older man. 'Fred; they could be waitin' for us at the camp.'

The older man scowled darkly. 'We got two more hostages.'

That did not seem reassuring to the tobacco-chewer, fairly young, at least younger-looking than other renegades Dave Petrie had seen. The gunsmith risked entering this exchange. 'When they're in place, you gents will have to sprout wings to get away.'

Fred, the gruff-voiced, thoroughly venomous-looking older man turned on Dave. 'One more word out of you an' I'll slit your gullet. Let's go, an' not a damned sound.'

The tobacco-chewer had the last word. 'We'll walk right into them, for chris'sake.'

Fred turned on him again. 'You got a better notion? No? Then shut up an' keep shutted up. Move out.'

Dave and the minister exchanged another glance. Dave would have bet new money Fred had been a soldier, but whether he had or not made no difference. Dave trudged obediently past and around huge old trees. It was a long hike but eventually two dirty, unshaven, lean, weathered men appeared dead ahead, each with Winchesters aiming belly high but not cocked.

Fred stopped. 'They was ridin' the rim when we got 'em,' he explained to the two men barring their way. 'Where's Len?'

One of the newcomers spoke without taking his eyes off the gunsmith and the preacher. 'Ain't come back.' He paused then also said, 'Are there any more of 'em?'

Dave replied before the gruff-voiced man could. 'Yeah, ten behind us an' another six or eight comin' from town.'

Fred turned slowly, walked back and swung a ham-sized fist. Dave went down like a pole-axed steer. The older outlaw stood looking steadily at John Kent, who returned the look only briefly, then put his attention on the unconscious gunsmith who had a trickle of blood at the side of his mouth. The older, gruff man said, 'Well, you scrawny bastard—you want some too? I got plenty left.'

Kent did not respond. His face was expressionless except for the eyes. Fred turned his back on the preacher in obvious scorn and asked if the two men who had appeared from among the trees had seen or heard other men on the slope. They hadn't. Fred jerked his head in the direction of the man on the ground. 'He was lyin'. There's no one back there than just these two. Get him on his feet an' let's go.'

Dave was a dead weight. The pair of younger outlaws got him up between them and dragged him along. They were not happy with this assignment but evidently no one argued with the man called Fred.

The cud-chewer behind the minister prodded Kent in the back. The preacher closed up the distance a little without looking back.

The little cavalcade stopped when the burdened men let Dave slide to the ground. Fred turned on them. 'Pick him up,' he snarled. One of the younger outlaws looked Fred in the eyes as he calmly said, 'He's heavy. You want to take him along, you carry him.'

For a long moment they faced each other, the younger outlaw unblinkingly challenging. John Kent held his breath. One of the other men sounded annoyed when he said, 'For chris'sake, you two, we're up to our butts in trouble . . . Settle it some other time.'

This outlaw hoisted Dave, growled for another man to help him and the little band resumed its hike, but John Kent, watching the burly older man, thought Fred was smoldering. He put his gaze on the man who had challenged Fred. He was lean, filthy, neither quite as tall as Fred nor within twenty pounds of Fred's heft. He wore his hip-holster not just lashed to his leg but the tie-down hung loose. The preacher made a guess; the challenger was a deadly hand with a gun and the other outlaws knew it. Fred certainly had eaten crow. Up to the moment when the younger man balked the preacher hadn't believed Fred wasn't very respected. Now, he paid more attention to the man who had called him.

Fred held up his hand for the party to stop again. He did not look back, just slipped ahead moving among trees like a tomahawk. The other outlaws seemed to understand and waited.

Dave regained consciousness, pushed clear of

the men who had been supporting him, raised a hand to dried blood on his swollen mouth, sank down working his jaw and focusing both eyes on his companions. The only one he gazed back to for any length of time was the preacher. He stopped gingerly working his jaw and shook his head.

The renegade who had faced down the gruff-voiced man laughed. 'You got to have an iron jaw,' he told the gunsmith, amused and relaxed. 'I've seen him put a fair-sized bull on the ground.'

When Fred returned he jerked his head and struck out. The others followed him. Dave got in beside John Kent who said, 'That was a damned fool thing to do.'

Dave was feeling his swollen face when he agreed. 'Yeah. Well, Preacher, it's not the first mistake I ever made.'

The man who'd been herding John Kent along said, 'Preacher? Are you a Bible-banger?'

Kent did not answer.

They were moving over a fairly well defined path through needles when someone challenged them. 'That you, Fred?'

'Yeah. Is Len back yet?'

'Hey, you done a good lick. Two horses.'

The camp was where Dave had seen it on his earlier trip up in here, only now it had mounds of saddlery piled in a heap, and a stew-pan ingeniously suspended from three green tree limbs. There was a small, dying fire beneath the pan.

The men halted, Dave and the preacher stared. Disheveled women were eating from tin cups. They hung fire in surprise when they saw the minister and his companion.

Not a word was said until Fred went to get a tin cup and fill it at the pan. As he did this he growled at the captives. 'Two more. Tie them two against a tree an' let's eat.'

The renegades who had escorted Dave the last quarter mile dutifully took both Dave and John Kent to a nearby pine and made them fast there with hard-twist lariat ropes. As they finished the lean man with the tied-down holster hovered a moment looking down. One of the men at the fire called over. 'That scrawny one's a preacher.'

The standing outlaw considered John Kent, wearing a slight smile. 'I'll be damned,' he said, and John Kent nodded his head.

'You will be. There's always room in hell for one more.'

The outlaw laughed, turned and went over to eat with his companions.

The rumpled, tired-eyed women looked at the latest hostages. The older women looked more disappointed than the young girl did. She was the age where miracles did occur, although she had to eventually wonder as she got older why miracles were such a haphazard affair.

The women were quiet. They might have thought if they acknowledged recognition of the minister and gunsmith the renegades might become trouble-some. Whatever it was that kept them silent might also have been the result of rough treatment. In either case they gazed at the tethered men in silence.

Gruff-voiced Fred finished eating, whittled off a chew and tucked it into his cheek as he regarded the prisoners. No one could ever mistake Fred for anything but what he was, a man with inbred meanness. It showed in the lines of his face. Mean and probably vicious.

He spat into the glowing embers of the little fire, arose to saunter over where Dave and the minister sat stony-faced. He stopped in front of John Kent, spat again and continued to study the prisoner. Eventually he said, 'I know you from somewhere.'

John Kent looked unwaveringly upward. 'You think so? I don't.'

'Yeah . . . Somewhere. It'll come to me.'

Kent ignored the burly man, who strolled back in the direction of the fire when one of the lolling renegades slowly straightened into a listening position and said, 'Quiet . . . You hear it?'

Fred grumbled. 'Hear what?'

The bad blood between Fred and that lean younger man showed when he addressed the older man. 'You're hearin' ain't very good. You don't hear 'em?'

Fred did not acknowledge what his companion had said. He regarded the man sitting straight with his head cocked. 'What is it?' he asked.

The young outlaw said, 'Someone's comin'. Sounds like they might be leading horses.'

That last sentence brought all the outlaws to the alert. The only thing that had kept them here was lack of riding stock. A whiny-voiced, rat-featured man with a perpetual down-droop to his thin, long mouth said what the others might have been worrying about. 'Suppose it's possemen from that town?'

Fred turned on this outlaw, 'Go see. Scout 'em up.'

As the outlaw arose one of the men left behind offered advice. 'Be careful, Sam.'

The departing man did not look back or speak. Fred remained standing gazing southward. He seemed to be wondering if what their latest prisoners had said about more manhunters being in the foothills might be correct.

Sounds came and went as though horsemen were picking their way among the trees. It sounded to Dave Petrie as though it was possibly a fair-sized party of men and perhaps led-horses. He tested his bindings. Hard-twist lariat rope didn't even soften the way other rope did when wet. All he got for his straining was sore wrists.

He was hungry and thirsty. He called to the men at the fire for water. All but one man ignored him. It was the lean outlaw who had backed Fred down yonder. He tossed a canteen.

Dave said, 'Thanks.'

The lean outlaw grinned. 'Preacher, good deeds'll get me to heaven, won't they?'

John Kent's answer was brusque and forceful. 'My guess, mister, is that what you been most of your life won't offset givin' us a canteen of water for your soul's sake.'

The outlaw laughed. He was clearly a very assured and confident individual. He let the topic die by putting his attention on the female hostages. Only the young girl looked directly at him when he spoke.

'Nothin' lasts forever. If that's Len with saddle stock you ladies'll be able to tell your grand-children how you was treated by the Mealy bunch.'

No one noticed how the preacher reacted to that name. He stared fixedly at the man who had spoken.

The outlaws were restless when, after eating, they should have been relaxed. John Kent half-whispered to the gunsmith. 'Where *are* those riders from town?'

Dave did not answer. Fred's hearing was evidently not all that bad. He twisted to glare at John Kent. 'Quit your mumblin', if you got somethin' to say, speak out.'

The preacher gave the burly man look for look until one of the men arose and ordered the women to come with him to be retied out of sight among the northerly trees. They dutifully went, the young girl the last to go. She turned several times to gaze at the lean man with the tied-down six-gun. He ignored her to roll and light a smoke.

Fred briefly watched them go, his face stone-set in a fierce expression. Behind him at the fire a youth who was probably no more than eighteen, lifted out an ivory-stocked six-gun to examine it for loads. Across the dead fire the lean outlaw trickled smoke, regarded the youth with tough amusement and said, 'Jimmy, you're pretty good with that thing, but let me explain a fact of life to you: There's always someone better. An' somethin' else, boy: In a showdown gunfight it ain't who's fastest, it's who's alive afterwards.'

The youth put up his ivory-stocked six-gun and looked everywhere but in the direction of the man who had made fun of him.

Fred growled impatiently. 'What's takin' 'em so long?'

The lean man said, 'Trees. You blind?'

Fred turned on him with a snarl, struggled with his temper for a moment then walked away.

The lean man laughed.

Opposite him at the ash and coals a pensive-appearing pipe-smoker addressed the lean man. 'One of these times he's goin' to come for you.'

The lean man smiled easily. 'I hope so. My paw was one of them old soldiers in the habit of bossin' people around.' The lean man paused smiling directly at the pipe-smoker. 'He's buried under a manure pile behind a log barn back in Missouri.'

The pipe-smoker knocked out dottle, pocketed his little pipe, arose and sauntered southward, the direction the scout had taken.

Dave had a suspicion since his capture that horse-outlaws set afoot in an isolated area of big timber were subject to cabin-fever, something that would not occur among them as long as they were mobile.

Renegades ordinarily left in clouds of dust after a raid. If Dave's captors even suspected he was responsible for setting them afoot, without a doubt they would kill him, Fred in particular. Not shoot him, that was too noisy, hang him.

7

Back in the Saddle

The youth with the ivory-stocked Colt spoke to the pipe-smoker. 'Where are Luke an' Walt? An' I don't hear no horses, do you?'

The older outlaw glanced southward before speaking. 'I got a bad feelin', lad,' and got to his feet still looking in the direction two of his companions had gone. His anxiety seemed to increase the longer he stood there. One of the other men also arose. He dusted himself off, then absent-mindedly reached inside his shirt to scratch.

The young outlaw came up off the ground slowly. He was the only one to break the silence. He sounded even more worried.

'I don't like this.'

One of the lounging men spoke almost fatalistically. 'I ain't liked it since some bastard turned our horses loose.'

Dave and the preacher watched an obvious slow consternation begin to spread. The lanky gunman spoke quietly. 'If them prisoners was tellin' the truth,' he paused. 'Fred an' Len was wrong, even if we had to walk it would have been better'n settin' here like a bunch of quail. We all should have gone with Len.'

Dave watched them. Preacher Kent did too, but not in the same way. There was the hint of a bitter smile hovering around his mouth.

Except for the bound men sitting with their backs to a large tree everyone was standing up, trying to hear or see what was beginning to trouble each of them. They only moved when a gunshot blew the stillness apart. All but two of them fled, those two, the youth with the fancy-handled six-gun and the lean outlaw stood fast, both with weapons in their fists.

There was nothing to shoot at among the big trees. Echoes of that solitary gunshot chased one another into oblivion.

Someone was staggering, bumping into trees, lurching toward the camp. When he came into view Dave recognized him as the outlaw Fred had sent to scout downslope.

Neither of the remaining renegades moved to

help the unsteady man. Neither of them spoke his name or said a word. They and the prisoners watched as the outlaw seemed to be groping with both arms extended for something, perhaps the camp. Once the man raised his face; it was contorted almost beyond recognition. He was within a hundred feet of the ash and char when he collapsed. He fell on his face, belly-down, and that was when the onlookers saw the widening scarlet stain on the back of his shirt.

The preacher spoke coldly. 'He was tryin' to get back here an' warn you.'

The lean gunman acted deaf. He was staring at the dead man. But the youth answered. 'Shot in the back. What kind of friends you got, Preacher?'

John Kent replied coldly, 'Sonny, you been listenin' to too many cock'n bull stories. He was goin' to warn the lot of you—he was comin' back up here. He got shot in the back because someone saw him. How else could it have happened?'

The preacher did not receive an answer. The tall gunman twisted slowly from the waist. Half under his breath he said, 'Son of a bitch.'

An eerie answer came from the westernmost stand of forest giants. 'I got to agree with you. *Drop that gun!*'

The youth obeyed but the lean man didn't. He searched for the man behind that voice, did not find him and smiled.

Dave had been impressed by the tall, lean man's

defiance of Fred. Now he was impressed by what he assumed was a total lack of fear. Whoever had addressed him was not impressed at all. He shot the lean man, hit him dead center through the brisket, and there wasn't even gunsmoke to indicate where the shot had come from. Just the loud noise of a gunshot.

The youth opened his fingers, the fancy six-gun fell and Dave raised his voice. 'Don't shoot.'

He might as well have been whistling against the wind. The next bullet hit the youth in the forehead. He didn't have time to flinch or bat his eyes.

John Kent called sharply. 'That's murder.'

He got a growly answer from among the trees and forest gloom. 'I reckon. I can't see no more of them, but they'll get caught.' Jack Gibbons the town blacksmith came from behind a red-barked huge old fir tree. He barely more than glanced at his victims as he approached the tethered men, knelt, produced a wicked-looking boot knife, slashed the hard twist-rope and arose gazing at the gunsmith. He would not look at the minister as he said, 'Where are the women?'

The gunsmith didn't have time to answer, two gunshots sounded from two separate places among the westerly forest. Gibbons's carbine was jerked from his hand, wood from its stock flew in all directions. The second shot was also too close, it tore a large piece of cloth from the blacksmith's shirt at the elbow. Its wrenching force half spun the blacksmith. He lost his balance even as the preacher dove toward the dead gunman, scooped up a six-gun and fired it empty into the trees.

When the noises subsided, a twangy voice shouted from the south. 'What'n hell you shootin' at, Preacher?'

This man too was hidden among the trees. John Kent lay beside the corpse plucking loads from the dead man's shell belt. He didn't fumble. He reloaded the six-gun quickly. What impressed Dave Petrie was the way he did this; entirely by feel as he scanned the westerly area. But they were gone, whoever they had been. That blizzard of lead would have daunted the most courageous of men.

For the time being it was over. Dave Petrie picked up the ivory-stock six-gun, gazed at its youthful dead owner and said, 'Two less.'

He turned to watch the wiry, rather slight minister and Jack Gibbons crossing in the direction where the preacher had watched the women being taken. Gibbons's arm was bleeding slightly. Dave shook his head; some men were hung with horse-shoes.

Silence returned briefly, before the gunsmith could hear nearly hysterical women loudly wailing, blubbering their gratitude for having been rescued.

He watched the women come out of the trees with their rescuers and wondered about the wisdom of five people crossing the clearing in plain sight where ten minutes earlier two separate individuals had tried to kill the blacksmith from hiding.

But nothing happened. The disheveled women were still close to hysteria as they approached the place where Dave Petrie was standing over the dead youth, the ivory-stocked six-gun in his holster, when the young girl abruptly halted, with both hands over her mouth, and screamed. The lean, debonair gunman was lying face up. Blood was no longer pumping, in fact it hadn't flowed more than a few moments after the blacksmith's bullet had killed the gunman.

She fell to her knees, still with both hands pressed over her lower face. Dave, Preacher Kent and the blacksmith stood like stones. One of the older women said something to her companion. They went to the girl, lifted her to her feet and turned with her so she couldn't see the lifeless, drying eyes.

At Dave's expression with raised eyebrows one of the women said, 'You wouldn't understand.'

In the distance there was a spate of gunfire, then silence. Men appeared cautiously, entering the clearing from different directions, all townsmen, all carrying saddleguns in both hands.

An older man leaned his gun aside, took the girl in his arms to console her. She was still slightly hysterical. He said, 'It'll be all right now, Pearl. No need to cry any more.'

It did not occur to him that neither of the older women were crying, had recovered from their earlier hysteria. But as he stood comforting the girl the pair of older women exchanged a knowing glance.

The last arrivals were three men riding one horse and leading another. They had a prisoner securely tied on one of the led-horses. It was the renegade Fred had sent to see where the earlier scout had gone. He looked demoralized; his face was bruised. Maybe he had put up a fight when captured, maybe he hadn't, but someone had for a fact overhauled him with bony fists.

Where they halted to consider the dead and the living, one of them leaned, spat amber, straightened back up and said, 'We surprised 'em; got the horses. There was more men but they got away among the trees.' The speaker was Gerald Shoup the saloonman, who now jutted his jaw in the direction of the first man to die. 'That son of a bitch tried to run for it.' The saloonman looked disdainful as he said, 'Danged fool.' Gerald didn't say who shot the man in the back.

The riders from Spartanville dismounted. They looked almost as wrung out as their horses looked. Someone complained that they were wasting time they should be using running down the renegades that were still loose.

The saloonman put a sour look at the speaker. 'Go ahead. Do it on your own an' on foot.' He faced the gunsmith again. 'How many is there?'

Dave had to guess. 'No more'n half what there was. That's a guess.'

'Well, dammit, how many was there to start with?'

John Kent replied. 'Eleven, countin' the one at the jailhouse.' He bobbed his head in the direction of the two men. 'Countin' the one at the jailhouse bein' out of it, an' these three, plus the one you brought in, maybe six or seven. We knocked one over the head before they caught us I'd guess he's still trussed. Maybe seven still loose.'

Gerald Shoup gazed stonily at the minister. It wasn't difficult to imagine what he was thinking but he didn't say it. He shrugged slightly. Maybe fighting preachers weren't unusual but to him they certainly were.

The girl was down to sobbing with her back to the dead gunman. The posse-riders leading stolen horses brought two forward, made squaw bridles and handed the shanks to Dave and John Kent. They shook their heads. Their own animals had been tethered in the trees. When the preacher went after them Dave told Gerald Shoup that whatever others thought of the minister and speaking for himself, Dave would never ask for a better man to ride with.

The horses that had been stolen wore the left-shoulder mark of a man named Mark Fenster. M F in a small circle. He was the owner of the southwesterly ranch Ames Boyd had mentioned and evidently it was true the other raiders knew about his place too.

Dave knew the cowman; he'd worked on several guns for him. He said, 'One of the bastards who run off from you is called Len. He's their head honcho. I don't know how he managed to steal those Fenster horses, but if Mister Fenster catches Len before we do, he'll hang him as sure as hell is hot.'

The women were impatient to get back to town. Three town-riders gallantly gave them their saddle animals and struck out with the women, all three men riding bareback on Fenster horses using squaw reins of rope.

Pearl Tweedy looked back once before the small cavalcade disappeared downslope into the forest.

As Dave accepted the reins to his animal from the preacher he snugged up and mounted. The others looked up at him. Gerald spoke resignedly. 'Our horses had a hell of a ride gettin' here, Dave.'

The gunsmith had noticed. 'It won't be a horse race, Gerald, those bastards are afoot.'

The saloonman had one more objection. 'Trackin' them in a pine forest . . . Dave only an In'ian could do that.'

Dave and the preacher exchanged a glance. Kent said, 'Do you have any idea which way they went, Mister Shoup?'

Gerald gestured with a heavy arm. 'West; we heard 'em runnin'.'

The minister went to his animal, swung up and nodded at the gunsmith. Those two struck out southwesterly. For a few moments the others watched before Gerald Shoup said, 'Let's go. Favor your animals, remember we still got to get back from here.'

The distance to the M F ranch would have been no more than three or four miles, if it had been a straight run, but it wasn't, the ride was in and out and around huge trees. It was anglingly crooked, but it was easy on the livestock, it was downhill all the way until they heard a distant gunshot, more echo than substance, and halted with the open low-land country visible past the trees.

Dave made a guess. 'They either run into a bear or riders, either way bein' afoot isn't goin' to help any.'

The minister said nothing. He was trying to guess where, exactly, that gunshot had come from, a hard thing to do when someone is distant and there is only one shot.

They did not ride out in the open but remained well concealed among the final few tiers of timber, holding to their course. Kent did not know the outlands very well and was interested in the Fenster place.

Dave enlightened him. 'Mister Fenster has one of those foothill ranges. He has more trouble from bears and cougars in one year than other stockmen have in five years.'

'How many riders does he have?'

'Usually just him, except during gatherin' an' markin' time. Don't say much, works his land and herd hard. Sometimes if it works out, he'll help the neighbors, sometimes they help him, but there's one thing I can tell for a fact, if he finds who stole his M F horses an' can get the drop, by the time we find 'em they'll be hangin' in a row from a tree limb.'

'Has he done that before?' the preacher asked, and got a dour look from the gunsmith.

'Folks don't talk about things like that. They do 'em, mostly they afterwards bury 'em an' that's the end of it.'

As the preacher ducked to avoid a low limb he offered his opinion of lynching. 'Someday we got to get some law in the Spartanville country.'

Dave's answer to that was dryly said. 'I hope not. Law books an' fee lawyers make mountains out of molehills. Common sense law don't have much to do with book-law. It's called justice.'

Kent pondered that for a quarter mile before speaking again, 'An' hang the wrong people?'

Dave's disgust was increasing. 'Preacher, when you know someone's stole your horses, that's all you got to know.'

The minister let the topic die. After a while he said, 'How much farther?'

'About a mile or a little less.' To prove his point Dave dropped down to the open country, but remained where the forest provided a solidly gloomy background. He rode a while then stopped and raised his arm without speaking.

The ranch was a close scattering of log buildings with round corrals out back. Everything was made of wood, which was no surprise as close as it was to timber.

To the minister it resembled dozens of other ranch yards he'd seen, only this one, even from a distance had an air of abandonment. Dave didn't like that, he edged back into the shielding timber and continued westward. He was thinking of the odds, three to one, and the experience of the raiders. He also remembered that solitary gunshot. Fenster was no different from other folks; regardless of his alertness and his handiness with weapons as well as his lack of compunction about using them, he could be caught by surprise.

John Kent rode with squinted eyes. The closer they got the less he liked his feeling of apprehension. Eventually, with everything but the rear of the barn and several outbuildings in sight, the total silence, lack of smoke from the chimney of the main-house, a peculiar atmosphere of something wrong, bothered him.

He had his shotgun dangling from the thong around the saddlehorn. He also had a six-gun in the front of his britches; it wasn't exactly fear that made him hang back, it was something less susceptible to definition—a feeling, a hunch, a premonition.

They halted in the final tree-stand to sit their sad-dles. John Kent said, 'Something's not right over there,' and Dave slowly nodded.

The minister made another comment. 'Don't he have a dog? Most ranches have at least one dog.'

Dave couldn't remember whether Mark Fenster had a dog, but he understood why the preacher had said that; there was no dog barking, no sign of a dog, no sign of Fenster.

Dave reined deeper into the trees heading on a half-moon encircling course to go around until they could see behind the buildings.

Eventually, when they were far enough west to begin another downhill angling ride, they saw the rancher and Dave stopped his horse. He also saw something else, a man with ankles tied, arms lashed behind his back, his head at a grotesque angle as he almost imperceptibly turned gently on the rope that had choked the life out of him.

That startling sight kept the watchers stiffly silent even when a man emerged from the log barn leading a big brown mare harnessed to a light wagon.

John Kent asked if that was Fenster. Dave nodded. They watched the cowman ease his inert victim into the bed of the wagon, limbs still bound, cover the corpse with an old canvas and move for-ward to climb to the wagon seat when Dave and John Kent rode out of the timber heading straight for the rear of the barn where the dead man had been hanged from a massive oak baulk in the barn's rear opening.

The man beside the wagon was lined, perpetually squinty-eyed, thin-lipped with a prominent hawk-like nose. He did not move. He stood watching the riders. He recognized them both when they were close, made an expressionless, wooden nod of his head and stood at the head of his harness horse as he said, 'You lads are a long way from town.'

The gunsmith conceded this. 'We got raided, Mister Fenster. We caught some of them but by my count six or maybe seven aren't accounted for. They stole three women and a fourteen-year-old girl from town.'

'Did you get 'em back?'

'Yes,' Dave said, while the minister gazed steadily at the silhouette of a man under the old canvas. 'By now or real soon they'll be back in town.'

'What brings you over here, Mister Petrie?'

'A few of them went horse-hunting. When we met 'em they had three Circle M F animals on lead shanks.'

'An' what happened to 'em, gents?'

'They got away. Maybe four, most likely three. Some of their friends got shot.'

'Killed, Mister Petrie?'

'Dead as doornails, Mister Fenster.'

The cowman turned and flipped the canvas. His

back was to Dave and John Kent when he said, 'I think maybe the number's been whittled down a mite.' He turned, solemn as an owl. 'They got the horses for a fact. I was fixin' to saddle up an' go manhuntin' when several armed men come sneakin' out of the timber. I was outside an' saw 'em. I figured they was after more horses. Anyway, I got inside the barn on their blind side an' when they come sneakin' like coyotes, I caught 'em flat-footed. Two of 'em run like deer. I tried a shot but the light wasn't good. I think I winged one of 'em though, the feller went down, scrambled up and run harder than ever, but he was limpin'.'

'Where'd they go?'

'Back into the timber. I was fixin' to haul the one I caught up in there an' pile rocks on him.'

Fenster turned to gaze at the corpse. 'He's too old to be in the rustlin' business.' Fenster held up a little well-used pipe. 'Before I hauled him up he asked if he could have one last smoke . . . I smoked with him. He didn't say a word an' neither did I. When he finished he handed me the pipe an' I used this same horse to haul him up in the barn doorway.'

John Kent was gazing steadily at the stockman. He did not look either understanding nor approving. Dave offset that with a dry remark. 'We got to go after the other two, Mister Fenster. You got any idea which way they went?'

'North up into the timber, that's all I can tell

you . . . Good huntin', boys.' The craggy stockman eyed John Kent. 'Preacher, ain't this somewhat out of your line of work?'

John Kent did not reply, he turned and followed the gunsmith in the direction of the timbered uplands.

8

No Rest—Yet

Neither the minister nor the gunsmith were trackers in places where layers of pine and fir needles took imprints of shod horses fairly well, but the imprint of a boot left either no imprint or a rare one.

All they had to go by was the abrupt turn eastward where the last sign they could read showed boot tracks in a light layer of dust a yard or two before the manhunters entered the forest.

Dave stopped there, gazed a long time at the tracks before saying, 'They're crazy to head toward their camp, but my guess is that's where they're goin'.'

The minister said nothing. He had already arrived at the same conclusion.

They entered the trees warily. There was a possibility the scattered renegades might have an ambush. There was no better place for one.

An indication that the preacher thought about

this was evinced when he unslung his shotgun and rode with it across his lap, held there by his right hand with the thumb resting atop one of the hammers.

Their first encounter might have gone unnoticed if the man leaning against a tree hadn't called to them.

He was fairly well bled-out. Evidently that wild shot by Mark Fenster hadn't winged the outlaw, it had hit him through the lights. Every time he tried a deep breath blood appeared at the corners of his mouth.

He'd been propped there for at least an hour when the manhunters came along. That was enough time to accept the notion that he'd come to the end of his personal trail.

They dismounted. The man's eyes were unmoving in his regard of the armed men confronting him. He wasn't angry or even exasperated and disgusted. He was perfectly calm and spoke with a slight drag of resignation as though he knew.

Neither the gunsmith nor the minister knew the man. Only John Kent recognized him as being one of the raiders at the camp. To Dave Petrie, who didn't recognize the man and made no effort to, what mattered was his condition.

He sank to one knee. He asked if the wounded man was in pain and got a faint, sluggish shake of the head. 'No pain, gents, just awful tired an' gettin' more tired by the minute.' He paused for breath before saying more. 'You won't catch 'em. Especially Len . . . Are you the law?'

Dave spoke quietly. 'No. I'm a gunsmith an' he's a preacher.'

The outlaw's gaze went to John Kent and remained there. For moments he made no further attempt at conversation. He was failing fast.

Dave recognized the signs. He spoke to John Kent. 'Any ideas?'

Kent shook his head. As a minister whose duties included visiting the terminally ill, death was no stranger. He regarded the outlaw solemnly. 'I could say a few words, if you wanted me to.'

'I'd take that kindly, Preacher, but it won't do no good.'

John Kent smiled softly. 'Why won't it?'

The raider's tan-tawny eyes were fixed on John Kent. He had come to the point in his life when he had no enemies, hated no one, didn't miss sunshine or good whiskey, had no concern with people he had known, plans he had made, hopes which had never matured, and he was dog-tired and getting more tired by the minute. 'Because,' he told the minister, 'it's way too late, Preacher. Whatever's bad, I've done at least ten times.'

'How about a family?' the preacher asked.

'Naw,' the man replied softly. 'Naw, Preacher, they think I'm dead. I had a feller write to 'em saying I was killed in a stagecoach accident . . . Fifteen years ago.'

Kent continued to gaze at the dying man. 'One question: Where did your friends go after they left you here?'

'After horses. They got to have mounts.' The dying man was noticeably withdrawing from his everyday existence. He would no longer lie nor withhold information. He was detached, disinterested, and tired.

John Kent sank to one knee near the gunsmith, removed his hat and bowed his head. He did not pray aloud but he prayed. When he was finished he looked at the outlaw. 'Sins are forgiven, friend. The Lord knows very well the weaknesses of humanity. He forgives. . . .'

'Preacher, you're wastin' your breath. He's dead.'

They got back astride. Only John Kent looked back as they resumed their manhunt. When they halted at a puny warm-water creek to tank up the horses and drink a little themselves, as the minister arose wiping his mouth with a soiled sleeve, he gravely considered his companion. 'What that stockman back yonder said about manhuntin' not bein' in my line of work—you remember him sayin' that?'

Dave remembered, and, guessing what was coming, said, 'It's you got to live with it, John, not me. Let's go.'

They left the little creek on a northeasterly angle. To Dave Petrie the fact they made little noise, none of it audible for any distance in the big timber, was important. He would have bet his life some of those scattered renegades were still in the uplands somewhere. The gunshots which had scattered them had prompted a seeking for cover. In that kind of men it would not invoke terror. They were not the kind that ran in fright.

He was right.

What he failed to consider was that desperate men afoot in a perilous situation, wouldn't care a tinker's damn about being hunted by horsemen, their sole interest was horses.

When that occurred to him he changed course, which inclined the preacher to ask why. Dave's answer was succinct. 'We'll live longer in open country.'

Whether the preacher interpreted that correctly or not, he followed the gunsmith who was going downslope past the final trees to open country. At least visibility was improved and safety too, but south of the timbered foothills there was rolling country. That kind of terrain had its own advantages to desperate men in need of mounts.

Daylight also brought heat, something they hadn't been bothered with until they were well clear of the uplands.

Once, Kent saw movement north of them. He called to the gunsmith but by then whatever had been moving was no longer doing so.

Dave's anxiety increased. If that had been one of

the unhorsed outlaws . . . He began avoiding arroyos. They passed places where desperate men might be crouching in ambush, staying beyond Winchester range. This constant sashaying used up a lot of time.

The day had worn along toward its end during their long ride. Visibility would steadily decrease. Dave was uncomfortable. All they had accomplished was to encounter a dead man hanging from a rope, and a dying outlaw. They hadn't even caught sight of other raiders.

By his estimate there were now about five raiders still in the area. They would try harder than ever to get mounted. After nightfall they would rendezvous, what was left of them, and do their damnedest to reach Spartanville, a long walk but certain to have horses which could be stolen after nightfall.

To the gunsmith this appeared to be the last—the only—way the raiders could get out of the country.

While he was in deep thought John Kent spoke from behind him and to one side eastward.

In his formal way of speaking, and without raising his voice, he said, 'Mister Petrie—up ahead.'

Dave had a bad moment. The preacher mitigated it. 'There's Gibbons an' the others from town.'

He was correct, even with failing daylight Dave could make out the straggle of tired men riding head-hung horses in the direction of Spartanville.

Instead of loping to make the interception the gunsmith changed course, riding on a long angle so that when the interception was made, he and Preacher Kent had favored their horses.

The men from town saw them long before they met them. The blacksmith, the saloonman and two others turned to meet the men they did not recognize for some time, and after the recognition had been made, loosened in their saddles and slackened off until the meeting was effected several hundred yards from the main body of town-riders, who continued on their way. They didn't stop, they didn't even slack off but every man had his head turned toward the place where the riders met.

The blacksmith asked if Dave and the preacher had found the outlaws they had been after. The answer was negative, they hadn't caught the outlaws, but they had seen one hanging from a barn baulk, and another wounded one who died in their presence.

Dave Petrie and his companion rode ahead, anglingly to join the others. There were a few questions asked but for the most part the ride was made in silence. The men were as tired as the animals they were straddling.

Darkness blanketed their world before they reached town. Dave and the preacher left the others, who scattered in different directions. John Kent said, 'The women are safe, that was the main thing.'

Dave did not disagree, he said, 'You're a good man, Preacher.'

Kent smiled a little. 'So are you, Mister Petrie. Now what happens?'

Dave was leaning across his saddle when he replied. 'Care for my animal, then get something to eat, an' after that try to keep awake to catch 'em when they come.'

Kent gazed steadily at the gunsmith. 'What makes you think they'll come here?'

'It's the only place they can be sure of getting horses. There are no ranches as near as the Fenster place was. They need a certainty, not any more botched guesswork.' Dave considered the sky before continuing. 'It'll be a long walk.' He straightened off the saddle seat. 'Get some supper an' some rest, John,' he told the minister as he led his horse away to be cared for.

The minister watched him walk away. 'Big odds,' he said aloud. '*If* they come. *If.*'

Dave put his horse in its own place with a manger half full of wild timothy hay almost as sweet as sugar, went into his gun shop by the rear door, lighted a lamp, removed a boot, let a small rock hit the floor, put the boot back on and went searching for something to eat. There wasn't a shop or house in town that didn't have a cache of food. The gun shop was no exception. Dave found a can of sardines, some stale bread a man could roll all the way to Denver without cracking it. He also found a tin of peaches. It wasn't enough to replace his hunger but it served admirably at deadening his most troublesome feelings of hunger.

He also rolled a cigarette and leaned on the counter in semi-darkness going back over all that happened since the last time he was in town. Before killing the smoke his thoughts wandered to Preacher Kent.

If he ever met that gruff-voiced outlaw called Fred he would ask him about the preacher. Fred hadn't seemed to the gunsmith like the kind of man who would be mistaken when he thought he recognized someone.

It would never happen.

When the first dog barked Dave slipped out into the alley after dousing his lamp. This time he didn't take his rifle, he had the ivory-stocked six-gun in his holster. Most men who might be putting their lives on the line would have inspected the weapon, Dave didn't; he'd watched the previous owner go over his weapon as though he put great faith in it.

He thought very briefly of the dead youth up in that clearing, but only very briefly.

The night was dark, if there was a moon the gunsmith did not see it, several buildings out front had very tall false fronts, but there were stars by the hundreds of thousands, they shed enough light to see movement by.

The barking dog was joined in his racket by other town dogs. They may have barked in response to the racket of the first dog, the one whose noise came from the upper end of town.

He wasn't ready to believe the marauders could have covered all the intervening ground between the foothills and Spartanville. What he had no idea about was the time. He didn't own a watch, but it seemed that he and the preacher had entered town with the other riders no more than maybe an hour earlier when in fact it had been closer to three hours.

He went up the alley northward, halted beside the last building, listened, eased around the north wall and stopped.

He had welcomed the first dog's barking but not the noise of other town dogs. He could hear nothing except the dogs, a few of which slackened off, but that particular dog near the upper end of town neither slackened off nor broke the cadence of his barking. Whatever had incited him to start with, was still doing so. It wasn't varmints; that much barking would have sent even the most audacious of them scurrying.

Some drowsy-voiced but clearly angry householder let go with a sizzling string of curses, topped off with a threat if the dog nearest his bedroom window didn't shut up.

He might as well have been whistling in a wind storm. He didn't repeat his performance, he probably had done the next best thing, put his head under a pillow.

Dave waited a long time. Most of the barking died, even the dog which had initiated the barking began to only intermittently bark.

When moments of silence arrived Dave strained to pick up significant sounds. He heard nothing, and wished now that he had got the preacher to go to the end of town where the livery barn and adjoining corrals were, but he hadn't, which right now seemed to have been a glaring mistake.

Under the present circumstances if the skulking marauders were in town, that was where they'd go. Down there they could get as many animals as they needed. Going through rear sheds and tight little corrals behind residences would take too long and might not be altogether rewarding; everyone in Spartanville who had a horse shed and maybe a corral behind their residences, did not own a horse. There were more milk cows in those backyard sheds than horses.

Dave turned back and more or less recklessly hurried down the east-side alley until he was opposite the livery barn.

Horses reacted to strange presences differently at night than they did during the daytime. Horses are natural cowards which may have had something to do with horses being endowed with more speed than other animals.

Dave did not attempt to cross the wide, dusty roadway. Bad as the light was, it would show up a moving man very clearly, but he slipped down the south side of the building he had hidden behind, and which happened to belong to the blacksmith. There was risk of detection there but only when he moved, otherwise he blended very well with night-gloom and the color of the wood siding at his back.

There was no sign of movement across the road. There was no more audible sound coming from inside the barn than was common to stalled horses who moved, shifted, sought ways to make the boredom bearable.

Alertness kept the gunsmith from even sus-pecting his theory concerning desperate men seeking horses might be flawed.

He eased to the southwest corner of the building where shadows from an immense sycamore tree partially shaded the smithy as well as the roadway. The shade Dave required and which the tree pro-vided was not a necessity at night. Nevertheless Dave took fullest advantage, not of the shadows as much as of their leaf and limb projections which formed a kind of variegated pattern of camouflage.

A dog barked over behind the unused jailhouse somewhere. This time when other dogs chimed in Dave could follow the course of whoever—or whatever—was upsetting them.

The movement was unmistakably progressing from the upper end of town toward the lower end—on the same side of the main thoroughfare as the livery barn.

9

A Showdown

A softly abrasive sound somewhere behind the gunsmith made him freeze in place. He waited a long time before the sound was repeated. Initially, it had no sequence, no repetition, no identifiable relevance. For a while, until it was repeated, Dave Petrie thought it was some kind of nocturnal varmint, maybe a foraging skunk, but when he heard it the third time, closer, it sounded like someone stalking him. Soft as the sound was, each time he heard it now, it seemed to consist of the sound of boot-leather over dry and dusty ground.

That someone might have anticipated what he was doing did not cross his mind. He felt certain one of the outlaws had somehow discovered what he was doing and was shagging him.

How that could be he had no idea, nor did he dwell on the possibility; the hair on the back of his neck was stiff. He was probably between outlaws in front and in back.

He eased around the massive trunk of the sycamore tree, making movement correspond to the whispery dry sound when the other man continued his stalk.

Across the road a barking dog was raising hell and propping it up. The intermittent fits of dogs barking had brought several lights to life throughout town. Two of them remained alight for only a short time, perhaps because only one dog on the west side of town was now barking. For whatever reason those places reverted to darkness.

Other lights around town continued to burn. That dog across from the gunsmith's big tree only paused to catch his breath. He was furiously agitated by something. It was during his intermittent pauses that Dave heard his stalker approaching.

He squatted and cautiously peered around the tree at the exact moment the stalker left the backgrounding building which Dave had also used for cover before reaching the tree. Dave saw him as a leafy silhouette but recognition came at once.

He eased from behind his tree facing the stalker and held up a hand for silence until they were less than three feet apart, then lowered his hand and said, 'You liked to scairt the hell out of me. How'd you know where I was?'

The minister was an individual who rarely smiled. He did not smile now, he simply said, 'I knew what you were going to do. I didn't much care about the odds. So I waited up the alley until you came out . . . Where are they, across the road?'

Dave didn't know where the outlaws were, he only knew that by following that particular upset dog over yonder *something* had gone down the alley and evidently had halted out behind the livery barn. 'I'm guessing,' he told John Kent. 'My heart's still doing flip-flops.'

The minister finally grinned. 'Well, how do we get over there from here?'

Dave turned to study the barn, the clear space between the barn and where they were standing, and said, 'Go back up the road a ways, cross over an' come down behind 'em.'

Without speaking the minister turned. By keeping the big old tree between themselves and the barn they got back into the east-side alley where they hurried as far as the dog trot between the cafe and its neighboring building, went down through there in pitch darkness, emerged up near the saloon, and paused to reconnoiter. Dave nudged the preacher. If the renegades were rigging out horses down yonder they'd be doing it in the runway. Dave led off. They did not sprint, they walked. On the west side of the roadway they passed into the west-side alley across a vacant parcel of land—and nearly spoiled everything when Dave stepped on the rim of a discarded buggy tire. The other side of the rim came up off the ground like a striking snake. It hit him in the stomach.

He doubled over gritting his teeth. Preacher Kent took the old tire some distance and put it down carefully so as to make no noise. When he returned the gunsmith was cursing a blue streak under his breath. Kent shook his head. 'Blasphemy won't help.'

Dave eyed the other man. 'Maybe not, but there are times when it's good for the spirit.'

Dave led off but this time he paid more attention to what might be lying in the weeds than he did on the alley. When they got over there with a clean sweep north to south, a light was burning where that agitated dog had been barking. He was quiet now. As Dave passed the rickety wooden fence where the dog had his house, a man standing in a narrow alley gateway stepped out with a shotgun aimed belly high. He got no chance to speak, Dave spoke first. 'Jack, aim that thing somewhere else.'

The blacksmith obeyed, but not right away. He eyed the minister and the gunsmith. 'What're you two up to?' he asked gruffly.

Dave explained what he thought was transpiring at the livery barn. Jack Gibbons lowered his weapon and peered southward, it was as dark down there as original sin. He hooked the shotgun in the bend of one arm as he said, 'Are you sure? Did you see or hear 'em? That's one hell of a long hike from up yonder to down here.'

Dave was ready to answer when a shod horse kicked wooden siding southward. Moments later a man cursing in a restrained way sent a message to the men in the upper alley.

The blacksmith spoke to his companions without taking his eyes off the lower end of the alley. 'All right; I'll go down there from back here. Nobody in his right mind argues with a shotgun. You lads slip up the north side of the building in case some of 'em make a run for it out front.'

Gibbons did not linger for a discussion, he started southward. Dave and the preacher exchanged a look, followed Gibbons almost as far as the north side of the livery barn, then left him to begin their easterly hike. Once, John Kent got close enough to whisper to the gunsmith.

'That's not a good idea if there's five or six of 'em in the barn.'

Dave ignored that remark as he passed through another piece of vacant and overgrown property before reaching the livery barn. That whip-snake of a buggy tire had made a believer out of him. He would never again, if he lived to be a hundred, go ploughing through an overgrown area that people had been using for discards.

When they were close enough they heard men speaking in hushed tones in the barn runway. It appeared there had been a delay; two of the stalled horses, which had been stalled in deep bedding because of their unsound condition, had been half rigged out when the raiders discovered that one had a bowed tendon and the other one had a fistula right where the saddle sat.

It wasn't one of those collar sores harness horses got from poor padding, no padding or a poorly fitted collar, it was a full blown fistula that drew flies in daylight and had an unpleasant odor.

The animal with the bowed tendon only limped

after being tied or confined in a stall for any length of time. In darkness and anxious to get astride this was not noticed until the outlaw finished rigging out and turned the horse; it immediately gimped on a foreleg. He ran a hand down the shank, felt the tendon and swore until someone in the darkness told him to shut up and get another animal.

Jack Gibbons in the alley heard none of this agitated exchange inside the barn, midway up the wide, long, very dark runway, but Dave and John Kent heard it.

They moved up the rough wooden north side of the barn until they only had to poke their heads around to see the doorless front barn opening.

The preacher had a six-gun shoved into the front of his britches. This was one time he should have had his scattergun. He nudged the gunsmith, leaned close and whispered.

'That's bad odds out back. They won't ride out front into the roadway.' Dave nodded agreement but it was too late to do anything in support of the blacksmith.

Inside the barn someone with a raspish voice was profanely urging the men who had to get other horses to hurry, something he did not have to tell them, they were bringing other horses from stalls while their companions, ready to ride, fidgeted.

Dave knelt, soundlessly lifted out the dead youth's fancy-handled six-gun and held it at his side. The blacksmith's dog had stopped barking, either because he had barked himself out, or possibly because, with his owner in the alley, he felt no need to continue his racket. In either case there was silence everywhere except for the hissing of impatient, profane men in the runway.

John Kent eased up beside the gunsmith, also with a six-gun in his fist. He leaned and whispered, 'I never could hit the side of a barn from the inside with a short-gun.'

Dave ignored that remark as he'd ignored an earlier one. His full attention was on the wide, dark opening no more than sixty or seventy feet southward.

They could hear men turning animals to mount them. Out back the blacksmith could do better, he was lying on his belly peeking around inside the runway from ground level. Even if visibility had been better it was doubtful that the agitated renegades would have noticed.

He saw men rise up to swing across leather and eased his scattergun around, waited for a moment of silence up the runway, then hauled back both hammers.

The mounted outlaws froze. As the preacher had anticipated, their intention was to leave by the rear barn opening, use the alley to escape. They were facing in that direction when Jack Gibbons cocked his shotgun. The outlaws could not see him but every man jack among them knew by the sound when a shotgun was being cocked.

Up front Dave and the preacher eased around, they had heard an abrupt end of the noise. They could see men and horses, otherwise the runway was darker inside than outside, so neither of them could make out details, such as faces.

The raider who recovered first from the shock of being stopped from fleeing by way of the alley, spun his stolen horse and gigged it straight toward Main Street. Dave and the preacher fired almost simultaneously. The desperado went off his horse sideways, arms flailing the air until he hit the ground.

The terrified horse almost ran over Dave and John Kent before it turned abruptly southward and left Spartanville with its tail in the air, frightened out of its senses.

Those two muzzleblasts up front caused the other horses to fling in all directions. They swung toward the rear barn opening; they would have run in any direction as long as it did not have to be toward the front roadway where the blinding, deafening, terrorizing gunshots had erupted.

Jack Gibbons touched off one shotgun barrel then the other one. That noise was even louder, the twin muzzleblasts made blinding light inside the runway. One horse dug in his front legs so hard and fast his rider went over the animal's head.

Gibbons yelled into the echoes. 'Get off them horses you sons of bitches. *Now!*' He had time to reload one barrel. He aimed high and tugged off the shot. Again there was consternation in the runway. Both men up front fired into the roof. A big powerful roman-nosed bay horse with little pig eyes and a disposition to match, bucked. He collided with other horses. He was head-down fighting with everything he had to get rid of the man on his back. He succeeded; the rider let go a loud squawk as he fell beneath the feet of other terrified horses.

The blacksmith bawled again for the outlaws to get down. This time he got immediate obedience; the stupidest outlaw among them had no trouble making the choice of being captured or trampled to death by fear-crazed horses.

They ran to the side of the barn where a bench offered the only protection. They were armed but at the moment their attention was on the horses, who only gradually exhausted themselves and milled like sheep, still frightened but not terrified.

Dave yelled for the renegades to get rid of their sidearms; for a moment it seemed he might not be obeyed. The blacksmith repeated it as he worked past the high-headed animals with his scattergun in both hands and cocked. Again obedience was prompt; at about thirty feet a scattergun made mincemeat out of people.

There were lights throughout town and men shouting to one another as they converged—very cautiously and armed—from all directions.

Gibbons roughly ordered the outlaws to open

stall doors and herd the horses inside. He emphasized his order by wig-wagging with the shotgun. The outlaws moved carefully, got the animals into stalls, latched the doors and were facing the blacksmith as the gunsmith and the preacher came down into the runway.

Not until they were close enough could Dave see that one of the outlaws hadn't dropped his six-gun. He raised his Colt in that outlaw's direction. Before he could tell the man to disarm himself a single gunshot from just inside the doorway punched the outlaw to his knees. He made an effort to draw. The townsman among the small crowd of them coming down the runway, fired again. This time the raider struck wood at his back and pitched forward.

The other townsmen knew who had killed the raider. In time others would also know, but Dave and the minister never asked who the killer was and were never told. It did not matter.

Dusk was thick, the smell of horses filled the barn. Dave stopped in front of the raiders. He could see them well enough at close range. One in particular held his attention, a hawk-faced individual with smoldering eyes and a wound for a mouth. He made a guess about this one as he jerked his head toward the roadway. The crowd that accompanied the outlaws to the unused jailhouse became larger by the minute. There were the inevitable murmurs about lynching but the black-

116

smith and his intimidating weapons squelched that. He stood in the jailhouse doorway barring the way, shotgun in both hands as he said, 'Not yet, gents. We got some sorting out to do first, then maybe you can have 'em.'

Among the crowd a man said, 'What sorting out, Jack? Them sons of bitches killed folks in town. Shot 'em in cold blood. We don't need no sorting out for what they done.'

Gibbons was adamant. It was too dark to see who that speaker had been, but every man being barred from entering the jailhouse clearly felt the same way.

Gibbons growled at them. 'Go on back to bed,' he said, stepped back and slammed the door.

Preacher Kent had found a lamp and lighted it. There was a ceiling-wire from which the lantern could be hung. By the light the outlaws leaning against a wall looked gaunt, unshaven, filthy and solemn as they studied their captors.

The blacksmith sat down, seemingly without meaning to, his shotgun aimed belt-high toward the men along the wall. He said, 'The odds been pretty well whittled down,' addressing no one in particular. He paused, then spoke directly to the outlaws. 'If you fellers got another chance, I'll bet you'd never even come close to Spartanville again.' He smiled. The captives eyed him in stony silence.

Dave perched on the edge of a dusty table.

'Who's got the money? Fish it out and put it on this table.'

One of the raiders glowered at the gunsmith. 'What money?'

The preacher, a wiry, physically unimpressive man, moved faster than a striking rattler. He didn't actually strike the outlaw, he slapped him across the face with his open hand.

The man's hat flew like an injured bird, the outlaw's head snapped back, John Kent spoke softly but brusquely. 'Put the money on the table.'

The outlaw raised a hand where the slap had made his cheek red. 'You son of a bitch. I'll settle with you for that. I'll . . .'

'Shut up,' the blacksmith growled arising with his shotgun swinging. 'I'd as leave plaster your lousy guts over the wall as look at you . . . Now— each one of you step forward one at a time an' empty your pockets on the table.'

They obeyed. Each man had a pad of greenbacks among the litter of clasp knives, bandana handkerchiefs and silver coins they put on the table where Dave was perching.

When they had all obeyed the order to empty their pockets the gunsmith made a leisurely count of the money. It was all there, money from the general store where the proprietor had been killed, money from the stage office, and two dog-eared Wanted posters for a man named Jed Brown and a man named Charley Booth.

Dave watched the two men who had been carrying those dodgers. One of them was past his prime, Dave wagged his head at this one. 'What've you got to show for ridin' with no-good sons of bitches most of your life?'

The older man answered curtly. 'Mister, I had nothin' before the war. Durin' the war I got nothin' but two wounds. Afterwards nothin' was left. What would you have done?'

Dave shifted his attention to the man named Charley Booth. They eyed each other for a moment before the gunsmith spoke. 'How many dodgers you got on you?'

Booth sneered. 'Find out for yourself, mister.'

For some reason no one ever understood the oldest outlaw looked coldly at Charley Booth as he said, 'He'd have had a new one, or got himself shot. He was fixin' to take the young girl when she was tied to a tree. One of them women bawled like a bear with a sore behind . . . I got no use for grown men tryin' that with children.'

For a long moment there was no further conversation before the blacksmith said, 'Open the door, Preacher. You're closest to it.'

For years there was wrangling over whether John Kent would have opened the roadway door if he had known what Jack Gibbons had in mind. For a fact the preacher and the blacksmith barely spoke after what happened when Kent opened the door. Jack Gibbons leaned aside his shotgun, grabbed

Charley Booth by the scruff of the neck and hurled him out to the mob. Gibbons then closed the door, dropped the draw-bar into place and stood wide-legged barring access to the door.

None of the men in the room who might have done something to prevent the lynching which took place shortly after the townsmen had their renegade, moved nor spoke although the outcries of the doomed man rang out until he was north of town with dawn coming, and left dangling from the thickest branch of an ancient and unkempt sour apple tree.

10

Whittling Down the Odds

Tired men waited until the remaining outlaws had been locked into cells then went home. It was while the preacher and gunsmith were walking northward, one toward his shop the other toward his parsonage, that Dave said, 'I forgot to look in on that feller I brought back.'

Kent's reply to that was spoken in a musing way. 'His name's Boyd. One of the raiders said Charley's name was Boyd but went by the name of Booth . . . Brothers?'

David did not know whether they were related and did not care. He and the minister parted near the upper end of town.

For Dave Petrie sleep came in his back room on a cot almost before he had kicked out of his boots. As he was draping his shellbelt and holstered six-gun from a wall peg, he briefly thought of the former owner of the ivory-handled gun.

He was too young to die. Dave sank back and closed his eyes. Too young, maybe, but as certain as gawd had made green apples—by dying now more than likely other people would not be killed.

As he was dozing off he made a drowsy estimate of the number of raiders still alive and came up with the figure of three. He was snoring before he realized that two particular murderers had not been identified, the gruff-voiced man called Fred and the man the other renegades referred to as Len.

He did not awaken until eight the following morning. He itched, needed a shave and would have taken an all-over bath at the shed behind the tonsorial parlor if someone hadn't started banging on his front door.

He growled as he padded in stocking feet to the front of his shop, unlocked the door and opened it. Gerald Shoup stood there freshly scrubbed and shaved. The only thing lacking was his lace-edged pink sleeve garters. He gazed at the gunsmith for a moment before saying, 'You look like hell.'

Dave gave a predictable answer: 'I feel like hell.'

'You better get your boots on.'

'Why?'

'Because that battered renegade you locked up is dead in his cell.'

Dave's eyes widened. 'How can that be? He got pretty well used up, but . . .'

'I got no idea how or why, I just know when me'n Jack Gibbons took stew pails over there early this morning, he was dead. The other ones across from him took the pails but didn't eat . . . That feller with the hawk-faced look to him said that wiped out the family; the dead one was the brother of the feller that got lynched last night.'

Dave said, 'Wait,' and returned for his boots and shellbelt. As he was tugging his hat into place he looked at himself in a mirror with wavery glass that hung on a wall. He couldn't remember ever looking so haggard.

There were several townsmen standing around out front of the jailhouse when Dave and the saloonman arrived. No one spoke but everyone nodded. The loafers would have trooped into the jailhouse but Dave barred the way and shook his head. The loafers retreated.

In the cell room men's eyes met and slid past. Dave entered the cell with the saloonman waiting outside. Ames Boyd looked asleep. He was on his back with both hands atop his chest. Both eyes were half-open and dry looking. Dave didn't have to feel for a heartbeat, Ames Boyd was cold to the touch.

He left the cell door ajar as he returned to the dingy narrow corridor to face the stares of the outlaws caged opposite the dead man's cell. The weather-darkened hawk-faced man said, 'He was alive when you locked us in last night. He asked what had happened. We told him . . . Told him about his brother gettin' lynched . . . When we come awake this morning he was lyin' just like you seen him. We called to him. He didn't move. He died sometime in the night.'

Dave and Gerald Shoup went up to the office where Dave sank down on a wall bench. The saloonman remained standing; he had a business to run. 'That's two less, him an' his brother. Folks want to know what you're goin' to do with the others.'

Dave's gaze went to the saloonman. 'Me? It's not up to me.'

Shoup's expression did not change. 'Around town they're sayin' you started this mess an' it's up to you to finish it.'

After the saloonman left and before the gun-smith could hunt up the town carpenter and arrange for a pine box and someone with a wheelbarrow to take the dead man to the carpenter's shop, John Kent arrived looking fresh. Dave told him about Ames Boyd. The minister considered his boots for a moment before saying, 'I'll do the obituary at the graveyard.' His eyes came up. 'Any idea where Fred might be?'

Dave shook his head. 'You interested in him, John?'

The gunsmith must have hit a nerve because

the minister's eyes briefly flashed before he answered. 'The one called Len and the other one —Fred—beyond that who is left?'

Dave thought the preacher had deftly avoided an answer to his question, but he did not press the issue. 'I got to roughly guess,' he told the minister. 'Countin' Fred an' Len, plus the three in the cells, I'd say maybe no more'n five or six.'

'Countin' the first one you brought in?'

'John, I just told you, he's dead. Died some-time last night.'

John Kent regarded the gunsmith unblinkingly for a long moment, then sighed. He did not men-tion Ames Boyd again, not even when Dave told him the dead man and the one that got lynched last night were brothers.

The preacher returned to studying the toes of his boots. 'I guess it don't matter how many there was originally, does it? One way or another they got whittled down. Someone told me there was fifteen of 'em.'

Dave corrected that. 'My count was eleven.'

'That don't matter either, does it? What matters is Fred and Len. If they got a-horseback by now they'll be a long way off an' still goin'.' Kent looked at Dave. 'Have you talked to the others yet?'

'No. I only got down here half an hour ago.'

'Mister Petrie, if I was a bettin' man I'd say they could make a pretty good guess where Fred and

Len went to, if they got horses. Men like that always got a special place where they meet.'

The minister arose. 'Anythin' I can do?'

'Well; I'd like to get rid of the dead one. If you'd look up the carpenter . . .'

'Be glad to,' the preacher said as he lay a hand on the door latch. 'I'll be back directly—after you've had a chance to talk to the prisoners.'

Dave crossed to the cafe, had a very late breakfast, went up to the tonsorial parlor for an all-over bath, a shearing and a shave, and later, smelling faintly of the French toilet water the barber finished up with, he got pails of watery stew and returned to the jailhouse to feed his prisoners. As he stood gazing at the dead man he remembered something: The outspoken bitterness of the older outlaw toward the man who had been lynched last night.

He took that man up to the office, closed the cellroom door and pointed to a wall bench. The outlaw sat down. He watched everything Dave did. He could have been fifty but if that was so it was remarkable; outlaws, particularly marauders, rarely reached that age or anywhere near it.

Dave spun a chair and straddled it. His first question was predictable. 'What's your name?'

The rumpled, dirty, older man answered promptly. 'Jed Brown.'

Dave nodded. 'Sure. But it's more believable than Bill Smith.'

'Mister,' the outlaw said without blinking as he gave Dave look for look. 'I don't give a damn what you believe, that's my name.'

Dave shrugged. 'All right. Tell me something, Mister Brown, that feller they lynched last night—Booth—you didn't like him?'

'No-good whinin' son of a bitch. I told Len he'd try to get at them women.'

'How long have you known him?'

'Len?'

'No, the no-good son of a bitch.'

'About a year. Len brought him to camp one night. He'd just shot a jailer, got his keys and escaped. Len come onto him ridin' a used-up horse he'd stole, so he brought him to camp. I told Len he couldn't be trusted. I might as well have been singin' in a windstorm. His last name was really Boyd but he went by Booth.'

'How about Fred?'

Brown pursed his lips and gazed at the ceiling before speaking. 'Fred was tough and sometimes cranky, but he was reliable. Him and another feller, a younger, tall feller called Cuff, didn't get along. Sooner or later they'd have fought it out. Fred likes his whiskey an' he was rough, but he was a good man in every way that counted.'

'Do you know anythin' about his past?'

The older man's gaze at Dave widened. 'We never asked questions. Like Cuff, I wondered how he come by that name but I never asked. Fred? All

I knew was that he'd been a Union soldier, an' he didn't tell any of us that, we figured that out from the way he sometimes talked an' acted.'

Dave said, 'You want some coffee?'

Jed Brown shook his head. 'Don't use it. I was raised a Mormon.'

Dave could not quite suppress a humorless grin: It was all right to murder people, burn towns, steal and pillage, but drinking coffee was a sin. He shifted on the chair. 'Mister Brown, where would Fred go now that the Mealy gang is busted up?'

'I got no idea, Mister Petrie. Like I told you, we didn't none of us talk about personal things. I don't have no idea where he'd go, but Len might know. Him and Fred was friends a long time.'

Dave nodded. 'Where would Len go?' he asked and got an answer that surprised the hell out of him.

'Ask him.'

Dave's eyes narrowed. 'He's one of the prisoners?'

'You didn't know that?'

'Which one is he?'

'The feller with the hooked nose an' perpetually tanned skin.'

Dave let a moment of silence pass before he arose and jerked his head in the direction of the closed cell-room door. Brown walked ahead; he even stood well away when Dave leaned to unlock the cell door. Jed Brown was far and away no stranger to jailhouse procedures. As he passed into the cell Dave told the hawk-faced man to come out. He herded him up to the office as he'd done the older outlaw. He pointed to the same bench. As the lanky, spare man sat down he said, 'I'd have shot you up yonder if guns didn't make so much noise. I can smell a lawman at a thousand yards.'

Dave straddled the chair again. 'I'm not a lawman, I'm a gunsmith. I've never been a lawman.'

Len eyed Dave as though he didn't believe him. His expression changed at Dave's next words. 'I'm the one who set your horses loose, all but two; one was too cranky, the other one could hop in hobbles faster'n any horse I ever saw.'

The hawk-faced man's eyes glittered. 'If I'd known that I'd have shot you, noise or no noise. You ruined us. I got a long memory, mister.'

An un-perturbed gunsmith replied calmly. 'Mister, if you leave this town under your power it'll be one hell of a miracle . . . Where is Fred?'

'Go to hell!'

'Maybe. But you'll have been there for a long time before I get there . . . Where is Fred?'

Len glared, his lips were pulled flat. Dave arose slowly and just as slowly and deliberately approached the bench. Len recognized the signs and was arising to meet the challenge when Dave's fist ground over skin and bone alongside the outlaw's jaw. He went down, sprawled over the bench and didn't move until Dave got a pail of water and dumped it on him.

He then put the pail aside, turned to steady the outlaw, and hit him again, this time in the soft parts. Breath whistled past the renegade's lips. Dave caught him, pushed him down on the bench and leaned as the outlaw sucked air. 'Once more: Where is Fred?'

Len looked up at the leaning man. He didn't speak, he shook his head. Dave sighed, returned to his chair and waited for the outlaw leader to recover. It was a long wait. Len looked like a drowned rat. When his breathing returned to normal his hands shook. He looked steadily at the gunsmith. 'You son of a bitch, I'll kill you.'

Dave's answer was as dry as corn husks. 'Now's your chance.'

The outlaw leaned over with his head in both hands. He remained like that until Dave pushed the chair back as he arose. Len looked up.

'I wouldn't spit on you if your guts were on fire. An' I'll tell you somethin' else—you didn't get us all; some night when you're walkin' home you'll never get there. You got my word on that.'

Dave leaned back to roll and light a smoke after which he crossed to the bench and handed the cigarette to the outlaw. Len took it, did not look at Dave, inhaled, winced and exhaled. Dave stood over him. 'I'll keep on overhaulin' you until you tell me where Fred is.'

Len inhaled again. This time he did not wince when he exhaled. He gazed at the cigarette in his hand as though Dave were not there.

The gunsmith snatched the smoke from the outlaw's fingers, ground it out underfoot and leaned until their faces were inches apart. 'Stand up. You want to kill me? Stand up an' try your damnedest. If you don't get it done I'm goin' to break both your arms startin' at the wrist an' working up.'

Dave moved back. 'Stand up,' he said.

'Fred's headin' for Four Corners. He'll lie over along the way at some cabins we use when we're down this way.'

'Which cabin an' where's it located?'

'There's four cabins between here'n there,' Len replied looking past the gunsmith, eyes fixed firmly on the far wall the way a man would do who had been coerced into betrayal. 'If he got a horse I'd say he's at the first one by now. It's about twenty miles from here in the trees half way up them same mountains. It used to belong to a pot-huntin' trapper. There'll be sign.'

Dave returned to the chair, thumbed back his hat and stared at the badly beaten, soaking-wet chief of an outlaw band. Len looked almost pathetic.

He mumbled a request. 'Another smoke?'

Dave made him one, lit it and handed it to the renegade. 'Tell me about Fred,' he said, settling on the chair again.

Len inhaled deeply and exhaled. He would not look at the gunsmith. 'I don't know a hell of a lot about him.'

'Where's he from?'

'One of the Dakotas. He come out years back with his folks. They took up railroad land.' Len's gaze went to the floor as he continued, still unwilling to look at the man who had beaten him into saying things he had never told anyone.

'In'ians got his paw first, ploughin' a field, then his maw when she was hangin' the wash out . . . Fred was sixteen. He joined up with the army. He said he wanted bronco scalps, an' I guess he got a whole string of 'em . . . Him an' me met in a saloon in Yankton one early spring . . . He helped me recruit the others. That's all I know.'

Len dropped the smoke and ground it underfoot. He fished for a filthy bandana handkerchief, mopped his face and neck, stowed the red cloth and finally looked at the gunsmith.

Dave sat still and silent. In the early days there had been *voyageurs* throughout the high country, at first they were mostly French Canadians, amoral individuals to a man, then came trappers from the States, hard, fierce men who gradually took over the booming beaver-skin trade from *voyageurs*.

They built log cabins to live in during trapping season, which was during winter. With the collapse of the hide and fur market they disappeared and the next wave of emigrants came, mostly cattlemen seeking good feed and lots of it. The trapper cabins were still standing, still in fair condition, inhabited by wood rats as large as a cat who made dome-shaped twig shelters inside the cabins. Some of those nests were belt-high to a tall Indian.

Len spat, wiped his chin and leaned back. He didn't feel defiant, he felt demoralized and ashamed. He had never before yielded to the pressure of enemies. He looked at the gunsmith as he said, 'There's a trail. First, there's a big old fir tree with a blaze an' one initial—P—cut into it. The trail's pretty good considerin' it ain't been used much. At the end of the trail is the first cabin. If he ain't at that one follow the trail that goes along the low foothills below the timber country. Fifteen, maybe twenty miles you'll find the second cabin.' Len heaved an unsteady breath. He stared at the gunsmith. 'Someday,' he muttered and Dave nodded.

'In hell, Len, not on earth. Get up.'

The other renegades were shocked at their leader's appearance but said nothing until Dave had retreated to the office and closed the door, then Len lied for all he was worth.

'He done his damnedest but I told him nothin'. He never give me a chance. I didn't see it comin'. I'll tell you one thing, that son of a bitch hits like a kickin' mule.'

The older renegade Jed Brown gazed dispassionately at Len. Maybe the others were fooled, he wasn't. He did not believe a word Len had said.

Evidently the other outlaws did because it was obvious Len had been in a fight.

Jed Brown knew from lifelong experience why men poured water on other men: To bring them back when they'd been knocked unconscious.

The older man eventually stretched out, closed his eyes and slept. He had already told himself this time no one was going to produce a miracle. Deepdown he did not really care. He was not just disappointed in life, he was disgusted with himself.

11

One More Ride

The preacher visited the gun shop along toward midday. Dave told him about his talks with the renegades. Kent listened impassively and left.

For the balance of the day Dave tried to catch up on the work he'd let lie during the trouble, but constant interruptions made it impossible to accomplish much.

He was sipping coffee from a huge old crockery cup with shadows appearing across the road when Jack Gibbons came in after visiting the saloon. The blacksmith accepted the offer of coffee, waited until Dave had set it before him, then said, 'There's a lot of lynch-talk,' and afterwards picked up the cup to drink while watching the gunsmith over the rim of the cup.

Dave refilled his own cup and leaned on the counter in front of the blacksmith. He said, 'An eye for an eye, Jack.' Gibbons's uncertain expression vanished. He had been unsure how the gunsmith would react to a lynching. He changed the subject. 'The preacher rode out of town a while back. He had that scattergun on his saddle an' a saddle pocket stuffed with somethin', maybe grub.'

Dave considered the blacksmith without speaking for a moment. 'North, Jack?'

'Yes. Care to refill my cup?'

Dave took the cup to the little speckleware pot atop his shop stove, slowly refilled it and went back. As he put the cup down he said, 'Did anyone talk to him?'

'Not that I know of . . . Some of us was wonderin'—did we forget somethin' up there?'

Dave didn't think so, but all he said was: 'Corpses is all.'

'Yeah. Well, maybe bein' a good Christian an' all he went up yonder to bury 'em. It might bother him, wolves an' whatnot eatin' on 'em.'

Dave asked the question which would reinforce what he was thinking. 'Did he have diggin' tools with him?'

The blacksmith pondered briefly before answering. 'All I seen him carryin' was a shotgun hangin' from the saddlehorn by a thong.' Gibbons paused and faintly frowned. 'At the saloon they said he'd want to give them bastards a decent sendoff, him bein' a minister an' all.' Gibbons paused frowning at the gunsmith. 'He didn't have no shovel.'

Before the blacksmith could pursue this Dave offered a plausible explanation. 'This time of year with the ground as hard as iron, folks pile rocks atop 'em.'

The blacksmith's brow cleared. He nodded, finished the coffee and departed. His purpose in visiting the gun shop hadn't been to make enquiries about the preacher, it had been to sound out the gunsmith on a lynching. He was satisfied he had the answer as he hiked back down to the saloon.

Dave Petrie's interest was in the departure from town in a northerly direction of the minister carrying his shotgun. He leaned on the counter fitting seemingly irrelevant speculations together. There was something between Fred the renegade and John Kent the man of God. Whatever it was a renegade knew about the preacher wouldn't be pleasant and could be damaging.

Dave had told the preacher what Len had told him about the likely whereabouts of the burly, mean-tempered man called Fred.

Kent had left town a-horseback carrying his shotgun—riding north in the direction he would have to pursue along the foothills to locate one of the cabins where Fred would be hiding out.

Dave rolled his eyes heavenward, sighed and

locked the shop, saddled a fresh animal and left town with lingering daylight, riding north. He did not take along the Winchester rifle. He had the fancy-handled six-gun in his holster. He did not take any food either; that was purely oversight. He did not take the rifle because he anticipated no need for a long-range weapon. In fact he anticipated no need for a weapon at all. He had to find the preacher before the preacher found Fred, not entirely because he thought a man of God shouldn't kill people, but also because the renegade John Kent was going after would be a very difficult man to sneak up on. Finally, murderous as a shotgun was, it had this distinction only at short range. Fred had a six-gun, maybe even a carbine and would for a fact be deadly with both.

The trail toward the foothills was easy to follow, there had been enough horse-traffic going in both directions to have trampled grass in both ways, going and coming, for a considerable width.

The gunsmith loped most of the way. He was more concerned with finding the preacher than in the slowly failing daylight. When he reached the foothills he turned westerly because that was the direction Len had told was the direction of the first cabin. He had a good set of shod-horse tracks to follow for several miles, or until waning daylight made it necessary to dismount and lead his animal in order to see tracks, which he did not do; he wanted to find the preacher, which he probably would not be able to do if he slowly followed tracks on foot.

He was aware that the trouble with tracking someone was that the tracker was always behind his prey. What Dave Petrie wanted to do was prevent a killing, possibly two killings, so he loped along the base of the foothills in the only direction the preacher would take to find the renegade.

He had plenty of time to wonder what it was, exactly, that John Kent would go to all this trouble, and danger, to prevent Fred from mentioning if he was taken alive.

Before the raid of Spartanville he and the minister had been nodding acquaintances; Dave was not a churchgoer and a minister of God would ordinarily have no reason to visit a gun shop.

Whatever only those two men knew, had to be very serious for John Kent to be hunting the renegade with a shotgun.

There was something else too: Preacher Kent had done a number of things while riding with the gunsmith that a minister would neither do, nor even know how to do; things other men would know about, particularly if at some time they had lived by the gun.

Dusk came slowly as Dave continued his search. One thing he did not have to worry about was being followed. No one else would know whatever the secret was between the minister and the renegade.

He had covered quite a few miles since leaving Spartanville, and since horses were not machines, he had to slacken off as the timbered uplands on his right became darker and darker.

Len had mentioned a blaze with the letter P carved into it. Unless someone was capable of night vision that information would not be helpful after nightfall, nevertheless Dave angled closer to the timber and occasionally rode among the trees but found no blaze let alone one with an initial in it.

As nightfall descended he began to have a hopeless and helpless feeling. He had probably closed the distance between himself and the minister; he had ridden faster than the preacher would have ridden; he was in pursuit with reason to hasten, John Kent would not have ridden fast, he had to find the blaze tree and if he had left town early enough he would probably have found it by now.

Dave halted once to loosen the cinch, lift the saddle to aerate his horse's back, and allow it to graze on a loose rein. Grass, especially cured grass, lacked the strength to do more than sustain horses which were subject to hard use, but a horse had to eat often, and cured grass provided a filler.

He rolled and lighted one of his rare smokes. The sky was dazzlingly bright with stars and a thickening moon. The cigarette blunted what would under different circumstances have made him aware of hunger.

He was oriented despite the poor light. He had passed the Fenster ranch about an hour earlier. There were no other foothill cow outfits for a good ten miles, not entirely because stockmen avoided varmint-country when they could, but also because Fenster's deeded land ran for miles.

He ground out the smoke, snugged up the cinch and struck out again, riding blind but still driven to prevent his friend from getting himself killed.

He rode at a slogging walk angling in and out among the nearest trees watching for the blaze. He did not find it, which could have been the result of darkness combined with the probable fact that being very old, having been made by early-day trappers, scars that would be noticeable in daylight would not be visible in darkness, particularly the kind of darkness to be found in heavily timbered country.

He tried to estimate the miles he and the horse had covered since leaving town, and came up with inaccuracies provided by the extreme difficulty of gauging any kind of distance after nightfall.

Frustration was inevitable but he kept riding, continued to examine trees, right up to the moment when he was sashaying back and forth from tree to tree and was abruptly challenged by a rough-sounding voice which belonged to someone he could not see.

The surprise was complete; Dave halted, sat like stone until the rough-sounding voice spoke again.

'Who are you? What'n hell you doin' sneakin' around up here in the middle of the night?'

Dave leaned with both hands atop the horn. 'I wasn't sneakin'. I was lookin' for something.'

'In the darkness? Get down an' be real careful.'

Dave dismounted. He stood beside his horse trailing one rein as he said, 'Move out where I can see you.'

The bodiless voice ignored that. 'Get rid of that white-handled gun. Be careful. Just lift it out an' drop it.'

Dave sighed, emptied his holster and ventured a question. 'Have you seen anyone else ridin' by?'

Again his remark was ignored. 'What're you doin' skulkin' around in the timber?'

'I told you—lookin' for someone.'

'Who?'

'The preacher from Spartanville.'

That statement seemed to have taken aback the man Dave could not see. Eventually he said, 'Are you joshin' me, because if you are I'll blow your head off. I'll ask you once more—what are you doin' skulkin' around out here?'

Dave shifted stance, probed the onward darkness among the trees and hung fire so long over an answer the other man swore at him.

Dave finally spoke. 'A friend of mine is up ahead somewhere. I'm tryin' to overtake him.'

'Why?'

'To prevent him gettin' killed.'

The invisible man was slow to speak again. 'Mister, you're not makin' a lot of sense. You been drinkin'?'

Dave's patience was wearing very thin. Whoever was in the yonder darkness was not going to pull a trigger; if that had been his intention he would have already done it. He started to relate his reason for trying to find the preacher. He even went back over all that had happened including the raid on Spartanville. When he finished talking there was no response. No sound at all.

He said, 'Mister . . . ?'

The silence mocked him. He tried again, 'Mister, we're wastin' time. I got to find the preacher.'

There was no response to this either.

Dave tried to penetrate the onward darkness and failed. He retrieved his six-gun, leathered it and started to slowly walk in the direction from which the voice had come.

Nothing happened, no weapon was cocked, no rough voice snarled at him. Nothing at all happened. He spent fifteen minutes searching and came up empty-handed. As he got back astride he had an uncomfortable feeling. Whoever had been among the huge trees and the darkness could shoot him in the back as he continued on his way. Of one thing he was certain; he had not recognized that voice.

A mile farther along his fear became something else: Bafflement. Not entirely about the sudden appearance of the invisible man who had belonged to the rough-sounding voice, but why he had been there in almost total darkness. It hadn't been the renegade nor the preacher. He knew their voices.

Eventually, reverting to his search for a blaze tree, he put the mystery in the back of his mind. There would be time later to speculate about the man's sudden appearance, and his equally as abrupt disappearance.

Some coursing timber wolves picked up his scent and sounded in their snarling way. It did not bother Dave but it brought his animal straight up in the bit.

He found the blaze tree!

It was huge and very old, larger than other forest giants, and it stood back only a few dozen feet from the final tier of timber. The blaze was as he had thought it might be; old, partially grown over with the letter P gouged so deeply it would require generations for it to be healed over.

He dismounted, his horse had enough slack to lower its head but layers of resin-impregnated needles had thoroughly killed off any grass or underbrush there had ever been. The horse nuzzled his way back and forth, finally gave up and assumed the hip-shot stance of a very patient animal.

The trail Len had mentioned was practically invisible. Perhaps at one time it had been prominent enough to be discerned even after dark, but all Dave could make out was what seemed to be a solitary path working its way among the trees on a north-westerly climb. Len had not given any details; Dave had no idea how far the cabin was up the slope among the trees, so he led the horse as he began the hike on foot. It was just as well he hadn't decided to tie the horse and go ahead on foot, those coursing wolves were still out there, silent now as they made a sortie in search of an elusive warm-animal scent.

It was chilly in the timber. The trail was as crooked as a dog's hind leg but it had one virtue, even the gunsmith's horse did not make a sound as they passed up the winding path over layers of needles.

The cabin was in a clearing. It was weathered, the logs were about the size one man and one horse could snake down here from wherever they had been cut, probably somewhere farther up the hill. It was the custom of men who built log houses in the mountains to cut logs uphill rather than down-hill.

Dave stopped in the final fringe of timber. The cabin showed no light but it had a small pole corral which, even by moonlight, the gunsmith could see had been so recently built marks of the draw knife showed.

There was no sign of the preacher. Dave speculated that he could be outside stalking the cabin, or perhaps inside; if he were inside there should be a light showing. Unless of course the preacher meant to murder the renegade in which case he wouldn't need a light. Shooting a man in his bed could be accomplished adequately from an open doorway, especially when the cabin was no more than twenty feet one way and twelve or fifteen feet the other way.

Of one thing the gunsmith felt reassured about, the murder hadn't yet been committed; he would have heard the gunshot.

He had to tie the horse now. If the coursing wolves came he would take care of that in due course, right now he wanted to cross the clearing and reach the cabin. If Fred was in there and John Kent wasn't, the gunsmith could achieve two successes; prevent a murder and capture a renegade—maybe.

There was no way to cross the ghostly clearing without being seen if there was a watcher. He reconnoitered and found that the rear wall was solid, it had no door and no window. He started his approach from that direction, fancy-handled six-gun firmly gripped at his side.

The horse watched his progress with interest; Dave was the only moving object. He did not hasten but neither did he hang back. Once he struck out he kept walking until he was within a few feet of the solid log wall, then he halted and turned slowly.

There was no movement, no sounds, he moved carefully toward the wall, reached it with a thudding heart and began slipping southward toward the jutting logs where two walls came together.

That same rough-sounding voice stopped him in place the moment he eased around the corner to the south wall. 'Don't move! Drop that pistol!'

Understanding arrived as Dave let his handgun fall. This was where that invisible man lived, and this was where he had hastened to when Dave had searched for him. Those freshly draw-knifed corral poles were the handiwork of the man who had twice now got the drop on the gunsmith.

The voice spoke again. 'I figured this was where you was comin'. It didn't make no sense, that business about a preacher bein' lost up here.'

Dave leaned on the log wall. For the time being he had nothing to say. Eventually though, he asked if the cabin-dweller had shown his bizarre hospitality to anyone else. The answer was about what the gunsmith might have expected from a mountain-dwelling recluse. 'No! They don't come here, whoever they are. I can smell strangers a half mile. I run 'em off. I don't need no one an' don't want no one. That goes for you . . . Preacher! What kind of simpleton d'you take me for? Walk around to the front door. I'll have you in my sights every step of the way. *Walk!*'

Dave was tired and disgusted. He obeyed the invisible hermit, or whatever he was, stopped in the doorway and finally made out the silhouette of a gaunt older man holding an old army carbine at half-cock. The gun bearer said, 'Come inside. Careful now. Take that candle on the table an' light it. Real careful, mister. As little as this house is I couldn't miss if I was blind, which I ain't.'

Dave groped for the table, then the candle-holder which was as cold to the touch as only stone could be. He lighted the candle and straightened back eyeing his captor.

The man was old, lean and dressed in a hide hunting shirt and hide britches. He wore old boots and a hat that no one but a hermit would be seen in. His face was gaunt, the eyes sunken and shadowed, but the hands holding the old cavalry carbine were as steady as iron. The old man wore a *parfleche* bag on an ancient garrison belt. People who made hide clothing did not give them pockets.

He finally gave another order. 'Set down at the table with both hands atop it. Good. Now then—this time tell me the truth. Who are you an' what are you doin' sneakin' around up here in the dark?'

Dave considered the old man, watched him ease off the oversized hammer of his Sharp's carbine and stand across the room squinting at the gunsmith.

12

Surprises

Dave and the sunken-eyed old man regarded each other over a moment of silence before Dave told the same story about a missing preacher, and the old mountaineer scoffed in disbelief as he had done before. He also said, 'Mister, there's two things in this world I don't like. Liars an' thieves. I don't know whether you're a thief but sure as hell you're a liar. There ain't no preacher up in here an' never has been . . . Start over, mister, an' if you lie this time I'll bury you up here. What're you doin' sneakin' around here in the middle of the night?'

Dave got no chance to answer. Behind him a voice he recognized spoke crisply from the doorway. 'He's not lyin' old-timer. I'm a preacher. You ever been down to Spartanville? There's a church in the middle of town an' I'm the minister . . . Leave that old blunderbuss where it is. You got any more candles?'

The old buckskinner answered sharply. 'No. If you can see me you got enough light. You don't look like no preacher to me.'

John Kent's reply to that was dry. 'You wouldn't know a preacher if you saw one. Go sit at the table and keep quiet.'

Dave risked twisting to look back. The preacher had his shotgun in both hands. He was holding it low enough so that if he fired pellets would spray the room. 'I said go sit at the table!'

The old man shuffled over, sat opposite Dave Petrie and did not take his eyes off John Kent. He looked venomous. Still in the doorway the minister said, 'Where's Fred?'

The old man's eyes widened. 'Fred? Who'n hell is Fred?'

Dave, watching the old man, believed his look of

147

surprise and rough answer were genuine. Dave spoke for the first time since the preacher had appeared in the doorway. 'That son of a bitching Len lied to me.'

Kent was quiet for a moment before saying, 'I think you're right. I saw you cross out of the trees to the back wall. I been huntin' a saddle horse in all directions for about maybe an hour. I saw this old screwt trottin' from the southeast across the clearing before you arrived.' The preacher leaned in the doorway gazing at the old mountaineer. 'When was the last time anyone came up here?'

The old man answered spitefully. 'Last spring. Feller named Fenster who runs livestock down below, come by. That's all, just Mister Fenster . . . Him an' me been gettin' along for years. I don't need no company; he's brought me a packhorse of grub from time to time. I don't need it—except for the coffee, flour an' sugar, but I pay him anyway, an' he goes away.'

Evidently the minister was annoyed by this rambling explanation because he told the old man if he was lying the preacher would return, slit his pouch and pull his leg through it.

The old man surprised both younger men by exploding in anger. He half arose from the table. 'You ain't goin' to do no such a thing. If you wasn't holdin' that shotgun I'd be all over you like a rash.'

Old the mountaineer might be, but age hadn't

taught him to control a violent temper. He remained half off the bench glaring as Dave and John Kent regarded him. He was as old as dirt; maybe thirty, forty years ago he'd been a brawling terror, but not now, not for about half a century. The preacher's tone softened toward the angry old screwt. 'I believe you. Sit down. All I want to know is if a husky, cranky man called Fred—I don't know the rest of his name—has been here.'

The old man blew up again, 'Are you deef? I don't know no Fred. He's never been here. I told you that already. You got to be deef—an' maybe dumb. I don't know no Fred, I never seen no Fred. No one called Fred has ever been up here. If he had, an' if he was as annoyin' as you are, I'd have buried him long ago.'

John Kent came over to stand at the table looking at the old man. When it seemed he would address the old man he turned toward Dave. 'How'd you find this place?'

Dave half smiled when he replied. 'The same way you did—with a lot of luck. An' maybe I never would have if this gent hadn't caught me down below in the dark. How about you? How did you find it?'

'It wasn't too hard. I had plenty of daylight to find the blaze tree. I knew the cabin was inhabited by the looks of that new corral. I figured Fred would be here. I wanted to set him afoot before sundown, then stalk him in the cabin.' John Kent put his attention back on the fiery old man, shrugged and returned his gaze to the gunsmith. 'Skunked, Dave. It's too dark now. We could ride back an' larrup the answer out of Len. Otherwise we'll be flounderin' around in the trees and still not find him. The key is Len.'

The old man had been attentively listening. The more he heard the more he understood. When John Kent stopped speaking the old man said, 'Is this Fred-feller a wanted man?'

Dave nodded. 'There was a raiding band of them. They hit Spartanville, killed Mister Westphal the banker, killed other folks. Four or five of 'em, raised hell then run for it into the foothills. Fred's about the only one still loose. The preacher here wants him. So do I, but for different reasons.'

John Kent was staring at the gunsmith. He was on the verge of speaking when the old man spoke first. 'That's who they was! I was pot-huntin' over to the northeast some time back, an' heard some men talkin'. They was lookin' for a place to set up camp.'

Dave interrupted what was surely going to be another of those rambling, gregarious dissertations. 'What did they look like?'

The old man's reply was consistent with recluses. 'I didn't go close enough to see 'em. I just wanted them out of the foothills. I expected to go back an' if they was still there, scare the hell out of them.' The old man threw back his head and made bear sounds which were absolutely convincing. 'It's worked before,' he said. 'I learnt it from In'ians before you gents was born.'

Dave went to work rolling a smoke. The other two watched in silence. When he had finished and was lighting up he addressed the preacher. 'Where's your horse?'

'Hid among the trees. Where's yours?'

'Not too far. On the edge of the clearing.'

'You want to go back?'

'No; but what you said about blunderin' around in the dark . . .' Dave arose, saw the way the old man was inhaling deeply of the tobacco scent and left his sack and papers atop the table as he and the preacher left the cabin.

They went to Dave's animal first. He then rode beside the preacher to the hiding place of the other animal. As they skirted around the meadow in darkness which was definitely chilly, Dave gazed back at the log house. 'They get kind of crazy livin' the way that old man lives.'

Kent also looked back. 'Not him. Some do but not that old man. If I hadn't been holding the shotgun the old fool would have jumped me.'

They were angling southward, passed the blaze tree and reached undulating grassland where the chill was greater than in among the big trees. John Kent made a guess about the time. 'Maybe two or three in the morning.'

Dave contradicted him. 'Closer to four.'

John Kent did not pursue the subject. It wasn't important. He said, 'Where is the son of a bitch?'

Dave had never heard a preacher use that term before. He looked at the minister. 'I got a feeling, John, that by the time we overhaul Len again an' take the trail, Fred will be so far away we wouldn't find him if we had wings.'

Dave let that lie between them for a while before speaking again. He had been rebuffed before but he tried again when he said, 'John, I come after you because I figured Fred might be more'n you could handle.'

The minister looked at the gunsmith from beneath the brim of his old hat. His face was expressionless. 'I could handle him,' he said, biting off each word and continuing to regard the gunsmith. 'Folks don't get into trouble if they don't ask questions; did you know that?'

They rode about twenty feet looking steadily at each other before Dave said, 'Yeah, I know that.'

The preacher raised his arm. There was sickly light along the far curve of the world. 'Isn't that Fenster's place?'

Dave nodded. The buildings were an outline in dark brown against the oncoming sickly-looking dawn light.

Kent dropped his arm, rode with his eyes squinting ahead. 'He rolls out early, don't he? What's he doin' with that wagon?'

Dave shrugged. All rangemen rolled out an hour or so before daylight. 'We won't have to roust him out for hot coffee,' he replied, and reined slightly more southward in the direction of the ranch.

They startled a band of foraging coyotes which had been in a small arroyo; they didn't see the riders, they picked up reverberations in the ground of horsemen coming their way.

They flung up out of the arroyo like someone flinging laundry in all directions. The tired horses threw up their heads and shifted lead in mid-stride, which jolted each rider.

It happened so fast neither man had time to do more than gasp. The coyotes were a color that blended with the new day. They were lost to sight within two minutes.

Dave said, 'Rodent hunting.'

John Kent said nothing until they could hear the small animals yapping so that they could find one another again. 'Did you know some In'ians believe the only way coyotes could be as clever as they are is because they're reincarnated human beings?'

Dave didn't know this, rode a hundred yards in thought until he finally looked over at his companion again. Preacher Kent was a genuine enigma; he was preacher-like in town, beyond town on a manhunt he didn't even sound like a minister.

Dave looked ahead where the strengthening dawn light was beginning to make things clearer.

He could make out the distant cowman rigging a horse to a wagon, which was interesting; when Mark Fenster went to town for supplies he used a light top-buggy.

With increasing cold daylight the cowman saw riders approaching. He stood beside the wagon for a moment or two before abruptly disappearing inside the log barn. He did not reappear even after the men from Spartanville crossed his yards, but when they rode around back near the wagon, he hailed them in a no-nonsense voice.

'What do you want!'

Dave halted looking for the man behind the voice. Daylight was improving but as yet there was no sun. It was like being inside a dirty fish bowl. He called back. 'It's Dave Petrie an' Preacher Kent from town.'

The rancher emerged from his barn. He was not holding a weapon but the six-gun on his hip had the tie-down thong hanging free.

He gazed at them without a greeting or a smile. 'Mister Petrie,' he said in that same brisk tone of voice. 'Seems to me you're pretty busy out here. Did you find them horsethieves?'

Dave shook his head. 'No. We come across one leanin' against a tree. I guess you hit him harder than you thought. He died while we were with him.'

Fenster didn't ask what most men would have; he seemed disinterested in what a dying horsethief might tell the men who found him. 'Didn't see any others?' he asked.

When Dave shook his head this time the cowman crossed to the side of the wagon and flung back the canvas as he said, 'Well, I did.'

They kneed their horses closer and sat like stones. Fenster watched them a moment before asking if they knew the dead man. The preacher nodded. 'We know him. He's the one we were lookin' for. His name's Fred.'

The cowman pulled the soiled old canvas back over the corpse as he said, 'Well; you didn't look in the right place. I figured they'd come back if they needed horses. But only one did; this husky, mean-lookin' one. I let him get inside the corral to catch a horse an' shot the son of a bitch.'

Dave had sat gazing at Fred with a feeling that now he would never know where Fred had known John Kent. He sighed. The preacher turned wearing a smug little smile. He had suspected the reason the gunsmith had wanted to find Fred. He dryly said, 'I guess we can go home now.'

Fenster unbent slightly. 'I got hot coffee at the house.'

Dave thanked him, declined for both of them, reined around and crossed the yard in the direction of Spartanville. After a silent half hour John Kent put an amused look on his companion. 'I've heard men say they had secrets they'd take to the grave with 'em. Did you ever hear that?'

Dave hadn't. He knew what the preacher was alluding to. 'I'd guess there's an awful lot of graves with secrets in 'em.'

John Kent laughed but let the topic die. He was satisfied whether the gunsmith was or not.

They were within shooting distance of town with the sun midway toward its meridian when the minister wrinkled his nose. He smelled smoke, which he didn't comment about because breakfast fires would be smoking all over town, except that this odor was strong with the aroma of burning wood.

There was no smoke visible though.

They went down the east-side alley heading for the horse-sheds when Lily Tweedy, the disillusioned mother of fourteen-year-old Pearl, who'd had hysterics at the raider camp at the sight of the dead gunman, stepped out back to fling a basin of water. She saw them about the time they saw her. She flung the water then stood holding the basin until they were abreast, she then bitingly asked where they had been.

Neither man replied, but they reined to a stop. The disagreeable older woman said, 'Folks wondered. Mister Petrie, they seen you head out after the preacher left. There was talk you two'd gone to search for a raider . . . Well, you missed the fun, gents.'

Dave leaned on the saddle swells. He was no more fond of Pearl's mother than was the general population of Spartanville. He said, 'Smells like there was a fire.'

'Well; there was Mister Petrie, but the fun happened before that.'

The preacher had been softly scowling at the old woman without speaking. Now he said, 'The prisoners?'

She smiled widely. 'It went off without a hitch until afterwards when the carpenter's wheelbarrow busted its wheel smack dab in the center of the road in front of the saloon. Then they had to carry 'em the rest of the way to the carpenter's shop.'

Dave quietly said, 'Who did they carry?'

'Who else? Them lynched sons of bitches from the jailhouse. Built a big bonfire so's folks could see good, and hanged every man jack of 'em. I made Pearl go out with me an' watch. She liked to have fainted. Now, she's still cryin' in her room. Maybe I shouldn't have made her go out there with me, but I wanted to show her what happens to bastards who carry women an' girls off.'

They left the woman staring after them, took care of their horses, cleaned up at a town trough and went to the cafe for breakfast. Neither of them said a word until they finished and went out front where an overhead sun was making things begin to wilt from its heat.

Dave fished for his spare pouch of tobacco, made a smoke, lighted it, inhaled and exhaled before speaking. 'They could've waited until we got back.'

John Kent was mildly surprised by that remark. 'No. They wouldn't have done that.'

'They could have, John.'

'Dave, it wasn't you they didn't want to see a lynching, it was me. Most likely they figured I'd be against it, maybe even cause them trouble.'

They parted, one heading toward the little house behind the church called the parsonage, the other one shuffling toward his gun shop. He barred the front door, went back to his cot and this time didn't kick off his boots. He was asleep within minutes and did not awaken until it was dark out and cool.

When he walked into the saloon Gerald Shoup impassively nodded and reached for a bottle and glass which he placed atop his bar. Dave downed a jolt, his eyes watered and Gerald stood across from him like an individual passing judgment.

Dave pushed the bottle and glass away. 'Do you know how many there were?' he asked.

Gerald knew. 'That one you larruped said eleven . . . Do you know how many's left?'

Dave leaned looking at the saloonman. 'One?'

'Yes, by our figurin' there was one got away. If he was the feller you'n the preacher was lookin' for . . . Was he?'

Dave didn't answer, he refilled the small glass, tipped back his head and dropped the whiskey straight down, he then put two silver coins atop the bar as Gerald said, 'You didn't get him, did you?'

'Why would you figure that, Gerald?'

'Well, you didn't come back to town with him.'

'You're right,' Dave conceded. 'We didn't get him . . . Someone else did. He was dead when we saw him, so maybe that takes care of the whole gang.'

Gerald unbent a little. 'Have another one, Dave. On the house.'

The gunsmith declined, he was already beginning to feel ten feet tall and bullet proof. 'Eleven, Gerald. Did anyone ever tell you that's an unlucky number?'

'No. Is it?'

The gunsmith smiled. 'It must be. There was eleven of 'em an' by my figurin' maybe someone might have got away, but the gang got wiped out . . . How did Len Bowie take bein' hanged?'

'He wet his pants, otherwise he stood up to it. There was an older outlaw who took it best. He looked me square in the eye an' said, "Mister, you ain't just doin' your town a favor, you're doin' me one." I'm not sure what he meant by that.'

Dave wasn't either but he remembered the old outlaw. On his way back to the shop he saw a motionless dark silhouette up near the Spartanville Methodist Church. It wasn't moving. It was a man's silhouette. He seemed to be gazing north-westerly.

Dave paused to watch. It was John Kent. What Dave had difficulty with was the obvious fact that the minister was offering prayers in the direction where most of the killing had taken place, the same man who had contributed to those killings and while doing that hadn't acted like any preacher Dave Petrie had known.

Center Point Publishing
600 Brooks Road • PO Box 1
Thorndike ME 04986-0001 USA

(207) 568-3717

US & Canada:
1 800 929-9108
www.centerpointlargeprint.com